At First Sight

There was a brief silence.

"What do you think, Hugh?"

A pause. "She is well enough to look at, if one overlooks her clothes. But it is you whom she must please."

Georgiana felt her face growing warm.

"Do not be so blunt, Hugh! Come here and sit down, Miss Marland."

Georgiana came forward, and as she drew near, the man rose from his chair. He was quite tall, she noted. But it was not until she turned to seat herself that she at last saw her hosts and had her curiosity satisfied.

Lady Estcott was elderly and dressed completely in black, but there was nothing resigned about her figure or her carriage. Her back was straight and her eyes gleamed with good health. And Hugh—Hugh was the most beautiful man Georgiana had ever seen.

REGENCY ROMANCE
COMING IN FEBRUARY 2006

THE EDUCATION OF LADY FRANCES AND
MISS CRESSWELL'S LONDON TRIUMPH
by Evelyn Richardson

This season, Lady Frances is obliged to protect her friend from Sir Julian. But who can protect her from his disarming smile in *The Education of Lady Frances*? And in *Miss Cresswell's London Triumph*, Bluestocking Cassie Cresswell must face down a local enchantress if she ever hopes to gain the favor of one Ned Mainwaring.

0-451-21730-6

A TANGLED WEB
by Amanda McCabe

The Dowager Viscountess Ransome simply must find something to fill the endless days of summer. So she invites a party of young people to her estate—and sits back to watch the sparks fly. The guests look forward to respite in an idyllic countryside, but what they find is treachery, secrets, and that most inconvenient bother—love.

0-451-21787-X

Lord Ryburn's Apprentice

Laurie Bishop

A SIGNET BOOK

SIGNET
Published by New American Library, a division of
Penguin Group (USA) Inc., 375 Hudson Street,
New York, New York 10014, USA
Penguin Group (Canada), 90 Eglinton Avenue East, Suite 700, Toronto,
Ontario M4P 2Y3, Canada (a division of Pearson Penguin Canada Inc.)
Penguin Books Ltd., 80 Strand, London WC2R 0RL, England
Penguin Ireland, 25 St. Stephen's Green, Dublin 2,
Ireland (a division of Penguin Books Ltd.)
Penguin Group (Australia), 250 Camberwell Road, Camberwell, Victoria 3124,
Australia (a division of Pearson Australia Group Pty. Ltd.)
Penguin Books India Pvt. Ltd., 11 Community Centre, Panchsheel Park,
New Delhi - 110 017, India
Penguin Group (NZ), cnr Airborne and Rosedale Roads, Albany,
Auckland 1310, New Zealand (a division of Pearson New Zealand Ltd.)
Penguin Books (South Africa) (Pty.) Ltd., 24 Sturdee Avenue,
Rosebank, Johannesburg 2196, South Africa

Penguin Books Ltd., Registered Offices:
80 Strand, London WC2R 0RL, England

First published by Signet, an imprint of New American Library,
a division of Penguin Group (USA) Inc.

First Printing, January 2006
10 9 8 7 6 5 4 3 2 1

Copyright © Laurie Bishop, 2006
All rights reserved

 REGISTERED TRADEMARK—MARCA REGISTRADA

Printed in the United States of America

PUBLISHER'S NOTE
This is a work of fiction. Names, characters, places, and incidents either are
the product of the author's imagination or are used fictitiously, and any resemblance to actual persons, living or dead, business establishments, events, or
locales is entirely coincidental.

The publisher does not have any control over and does not assume any
responsibility for author or third-party Web sites or their content.

In memory of
Georgia Merchant Lance,
who shared her copy of
Pride and Prejudice
with her grateful granddaughter.

Chapter One

"**A**unt Estcott, did you bring me here to tell me you are *adopting a ward*?"

Lord Ryburn strode up to his great-aunt's chair, where he stopped, planted his dusty boots firmly on her Aubusson rug, and stared at her in consternation.

Lord Ryburn was an impressive sight. From his fashionably snug, buff pantaloons to the nice breadth of his shoulders beneath his excellently tailored coat, from his crisp, closely cut tawny curls to the look of steely determination in his golden eyes, he was enough to make a brave man hesitate.

Lady Estcott, by no means intimidated, gave him a quelling look over her spectacles and scarcely missed a stitch in the seat cover she was embroidering.

"You sound displeased, Hugh. I seem to recall

your urging me to find something to occupy my time—to make myself feel useful. And so I have."

"But to take in a ward! Some unknown girl with no upbringing, no fortune, no family! You cannot know the least thing about her!"

"Oh, calm yourself and sit down. Do you think I am that foolish? Sit!"

Hugh reluctantly did as she asked, taking the empty chair on her left. In the other chair sat Aunt Estcott's longtime companion and cousin, Miss Marigold Frey, who had stayed intent on her needlework through the whole of the confrontation.

"My man of affairs located her," Aunt Estcott said. "I required him to check her background, of course."

"Favington? I do not know why you keep him. I shall have my man look over the girl's—"

"You shall do no such thing. Favington is perfectly capable. And before you whip yourself into an even greater frenzy, the girl is a family connection—which you would know had you listened to me in the first place—and she *does* have expectations. I intend to dower her and find her a suitable husband."

Hugh let out an exasperated sigh. "Aunt, you are acting too hastily. You have not even met her!"

"I know what I am doing, Hugh." Aunt Estcott continued her embroidery with calm deliberation. "She is Captain Marland's child. I must thank Marigold for thinking of him—I had forgotten him entirely! That was very clever of you, Marigold."

"Thank you." Marigold blushed a little and stayed bent over her embroidery.

"He was before your time, of course," Lady Estcott continued to Hugh, "and I doubt you have heard of him. He is connected to me on my mother's side. He died a number of years ago and left a daughter, who has been living at a Miss Silby's Academy for Young Ladies here in town—somewhere on Church Street, I believe. With a little instruction and a small dowry, she should be suitable for a gentleman of modest expectations. There is nothing objectionable in my taking her in that I can find, unless you are coveting my fortune."

"Do not be nonsensical, Aunt. Of course I do not covet your money. I certainly do not object to your helping this girl in a reasonable way. But what of her mother?"

"Dead. That is what I am given to understand. Miss Marland has been supporting herself by teaching at the academy—and *that* is the very worst I can discover about her."

"She is *employed*? And you do not find *that* objectionable?" Hugh sighed despondently and sank back in his chair. "Could you not make her a maid or a governess or some such thing? God knows I wish you to be happy, Aunt. But you have been urging

3

me to find a superior young woman to marry for ages, and now that I am doing so, you are intent upon entertaining the gossipmongers. A scandal is something that neither of us like."

"Bah. You are the son of Earl Wyndgrave. You have nothing to worry about. You have a pretty fortune, a pretty face, and very pretty assets. Do not make silly threats."

Hugh said nothing.

"At seven-and-twenty, you are entirely too young to fancy yourself superior to me, young man. Your sex is but a very small advantage, and in a great many ways, it is a disadvantage—so do not contradict me."

"I am not contradicting you, Aunt. But I distinctly recall your informing me that I was *old* for matrimony."

"That is an entirely different thing. Being old enough to marry has nothing to do with one's wisdom. You have many years yet to grow wiser."

"That seems to support my posture of waiting to wed. I should not wish to make a mistake."

"Do not worry. I shall not let you. But I can attend to that and my own interests, as well. You shall marry, and within the season, Hugh."

Hugh did not answer.

"We shall find you a worthy young woman with good breeding and a good mind. It is extremely important for a wife to have a good mind, Hugh."

Hugh let out a breath. "That was my very first thought, of course," he murmured wryly.

Lady Estcott either did not hear him, or she chose to ignore him.

"I had no children, as you know. When my husband was alive I used to keep busy managing him, God knows. If I had not kept apprised of all of his little activities, he would have given a fortune away to his mistresses. *I* am wise enough to attend to such things, much to my dear departed Lord Estcott's good fortune. But I have become deadly bored now that he is gone."

"Precisely, Aunt. That is why I suggested—"

"No more about your suggestions!" Aunt Estcott let her work fall into her lap and fixed her great-nephew with an accusatory stare.

"I need something that will exercise *all* of my talents and *all* of my knowledge. I shan't sponsor suppers to raise money for old knife-grinders or some such foolish thing you think old ladies should like. This young woman is just the challenge I need. You may help me, Hugh—" Here she punctuated her words with her threaded needle, jabbing it fiercely in Hugh's direction. "But if you do not, I shall not see you."

Hugh sighed again. He was silent for several moments, drumming his fingers lightly on the arm of the chair and staring off in the direction of the oriental fire screen.

"Very well. I shall be at hand. But I shall not be held responsible when you are overtaken by scandal. And *that* is my final word!"

*   *   *

March 9, 1810

I have been the recipient of a most unusual letter. A Lady Estcott, a personage completely unknown to me, and one of some importance, has written to me stating she is some sort of relation to me. I can hardly fathom it. She must be a very fine lady for she wrote on such excellent vellum imprinted with her initials, and Mrs. Snatcher kept the letter a full day before informing me of it, during which time I suppose she tried to read it before a candle, for the seal had fallen off.

Lady Estcott has invited me to come to her, and if I understand her correctly, I believe there is a promise of a position with her. Mrs. Snatcher said she is considering whether or not I ought to go. Mrs. Snatcher may not be happy, but I am not so foolish as to let such an opportunity pass me by without availing myself of it. I cannot think how it could be worse for me there than it is here at Miss Silby's.

Georgiana paused over her journal and let her gaze rest unseeing on the candle flame. It was cold in her garret room, and she had wrapped herself in her old woolen shawl. The grate was unlit, as she was given very little coal, but Georgiana felt fortunate to have her own room, small and meanly furnished though it was. She had once been a student residing in one of the large rooms with all the other girls, and her promotion to instructress had brought with it this little haven of privacy. It even had a small window, although it was grimy and never opened; it would let in smoke and the noise from the street otherwise.

Eight years. She had been at Miss Silby's Academy for Young Ladies for eight years. It had been three years since she heard from her mother, her last letter saying there would be no more money and that Georgiana had best support herself.

Georgiana had finally allowed herself to believe that her mother was dead. There would seem no other reason for the long silence.

Georgiana closed her eyes, and the rosy glow of the candle flame played through her lids. She began to draw forth from memory her mother's pretty, smiling face, her dark and glossy hair, and the rippling sound of her laugh. *Why had her mother placed her here and then abandoned her? Had she become ill? Or had she simply tired of having a daughter to care for?*

Georgiana opened her eyes once more. It did not matter any longer. She was a young woman left to win her way by her own wits, and if Lady Estcott wanted her to come, she would go. Her past would not interfere with this new life—she would not let it. To think that she might live in a grand home with warmth and servants and good food! And if she won Lady Estcott's affection, what else might be in store for her? And yet . . . one could not sup on dreams or fashion a future of promises.

Georgiana focused on the candle and saw that it was burning very low. Mrs. Snatcher was as frugal with candles as she was with coal; only the teachers had candles for their rooms, and each candle must be made to last or one would be left to seek her bed in the dark.

Georgiana dipped her quill into the ink, then carefully wrote one final line:

I am now fully fixed on leaving, and I shall give my notice tomorrow.

* * *

A fortnight after the receipt of the letter, Miss Georgiana Marland found herself borne to Lady Estcott's residence. Georgiana was amazed by the lady's carriage, an elegant vehicle painted shiny black with yellow trim and with velvet seats within; however, that was nothing compared to what she felt when at last she was let down in Park Lane and stood gazing at the residence that she was to call home.

Lady Estcott lived in a soaring, bow-fronted town house surrounded with wrought iron fencing across from the expansive Hyde Park. Confined to Miss Silby's since age eleven, Georgiana had no exposure to this kind of elegance. It was all she could do not to continually turn her head and goggle at her surroundings. She thought the footman would surely find her amusingly simple if she did. He was conducting her through the gate, and she made an effort to keep her eyes on the path instead of gazing upward to count the many tall windows that fronted each story above her.

They mounted the front steps, and at the footman's knock, a stern gentleman in neat, dark garb opened the door. He examined her dispassionately as the footman announced her.

"Miss Marland to see Lady Estcott."

"Her ladyship is expecting you. Follow me, Miss Marland."

He led Georgiana to a parlor just past the stairs, bade her sit, and then departed.

Georgiana gazed eagerly about as soon as she was alone. The hall was narrow and long, ending in this parlor, which seemed to serve as an elegant little library. There were several richly upholstered chairs, a small reading table, and built-in shelves holding a variety of books. To the rear of the parlor was a deep window that gave a view of the small kitchen garden, a picturesque planting of shrubbery, and the carriage house beyond.

There was a highly polished brass candelabrum on the reading table. Georgiana gazed at it. Reflected in the curve of smooth metal, she saw her own face, foolishly distorted and molelike, as though her nose had been stretched to a comical length. She reached out and delicately touched its golden surface.

"Miss Marland?"

Georgiana jumped and quickly withdrew her hand, snapping her gaze to the doorway. A maidservant stood there, watching her impassively.

"Yes."

"Follow me, please."

Georgiana nervously smoothed her skirts as she stood, straightened her Sunday-best shawl and bonnet, and followed the maid. They exited the library and took the stairs. At the second floor the maid turned toward the front of the house and knocked on the first door they faced. At the summons from within, she opened the door and showed Georgiana into the room.

"Miss Marland, ma'am." The maid curtsied.

"Very well, you may go."

Georgiana stood still. She was in a very large, elegant room that she thought must take up half the upstairs. It was in the front of the house, so one side of the room was made up of two sets of bay windows, each set forming a crescent-shaped nook containing several comfortable chairs. The walls were a dark red that contrasted with the creamy white ceiling covered with ornate carving, and gilt-framed paintings hung between the windows and upon the other walls. She saw a fireplace made of carved red

marble on the near inside wall; the floor was covered
with an enormous Turkish rug of a red, gold, and
black design. Finally, a man and a woman sat gazing
at her from the nearest window nook.

"Come closer, my dear, and let us look at you,"
came the woman's voice. It was a mature voice, yet
strong and clear. As the light behind the two people
threw them into silhouette, Georgiana could not
make out any more of either of them. She stepped
forward slowly, halted, and then curtsied.

There was a brief silence.

"What do you think, Hugh?"

A pause. "She is well enough to look at, if one
overlooks her clothes. But it is you whom she must
please."

Georgiana felt her face growing warm.

"Do not be so blunt, Hugh! Come here and sit
down, Miss Marland."

Georgiana came forward, and as she drew near,
the man rose from his chair. He was quite tall, she
noted. But it was not until she turned to seat herself
that she at last saw her hosts and had her curiosity
satisfied.

Lady Estcott was elderly and dressed completely
in black, but there was nothing resigned about her
figure or her carriage. Her back was straight and her
eyes gleamed with good health. And Hugh—Hugh
was the most beautiful man Georgiana had ever seen.

Georgiana sank into her chair and tried to school

her eyes away from the gentleman. He resumed his chair by Lady Estcott and, his long and well-manicured hands resting on his knees, gazed at her with very striking, sherry-colored eyes.

"Take off your bonnet, my dear."

At Lady Estcott's command, Georgiana shakily untied her bonnet and removed it, all the while conscious of the penetrating stares of her ladyship and the gentleman. Beneath her bonnet, her long black hair was tightly confined by pins; she hoped it would stay in place.

"I am Lady Estcott. Here with me is Lord Ryburn, my great-nephew. I asked him to help welcome you to your new home. Are you pleased with it?"

What could she say? Georgiana had seen nothing with which she could *not* be pleased. She had never set foot in such a great establishment in all her life. "I think it is very—very pleasing, ma'am."

"I am very happy that you approve. I had hoped that you would. I want you to be very comfortable and happy here."

"Yes, ma'am."

"Now, I should like to know more about your family. Your father is a distant relation of mine, as you know from my letter. I know that he died young—some sort of accident, I believe."

"A mast fell on him, ma'am."

"Mm. Yes. I recall something of the sort. What became of you then?"

It was painful to remember, and Georgiana was uncertain how much to tell. She and her mother had been alone for a time, but then there had been a gentleman who frequently came calling, and Georgiana had found herself spending more and more days alone with her nurse. She had missed her father's laughter and his taking her upon his lap to tell her stories most of all. She missed his smell, that of faint smoke and brandy and something uniquely his. She missed his sweeping her up into the air and calling her "My princess."

"I stayed with my mother . . . until she sent me to Miss Silby's Academy. I was quite young then. I was just eleven."

"And how old are you now?"

"I am nineteen, ma'am."

"What became of your mother?"

Georgiana felt a twinge of nervousness. What should she say of her mother? She did not know where her mother's path had led her, and it was perhaps best not to know. She guessed that it would not serve her for Lady Estcott to think poorly of Mrs. Marland, and surely Georgiana's last memories of her mother might be viewed with disfavor. Georgiana's chosen belief of her mother's fate would best serve her here.

"She is dead."

"As I thought. And this is why you have been teaching at the school?"

"Yes. I had to make my own way, and fortunately I could. I am able to teach reading, writing, household economics, drawing, music, geography, and French, ma'am."

"Geography and French! How interesting. I had no idea those subjects were taught to girls in such establishments."

"Miss Silby has an interest in academic subjects, so she teaches some of them."

"You must have excelled in your lessons, then."

"Those that I am able to teach I learned well enough."

"And what of etiquette and dancing?"

Georgiana swallowed. "We were taught but little of those subjects."

"Little? Dear me. Those are very important for young girls. What is this Miss Silby thinking?"

"She is probably thinking," Lord Ryburn said suddenly, "that her students would need to make a living for themselves. Etiquette and dancing are not beneficial to all classes of young ladies."

Georgiana felt lower and lower, and fastened her gaze on the colorful pattern of the carpet at her feet.

"You do not need to instruct me, Hugh. I know what kind of establishment Miss Silby's is. I am merely confirming my beliefs. So, Miss Marland, it seems that you have some things to learn. There is no harm in that. I shall see to it all, and Lord Ryburn will assist."

Georgiana looked up in surprise. "But what am I

to do, Lady Estcott? Am I not to have work? I cannot think why I should need to know how to dance!"

Lady Estcott frowned and leaned forward. "Young woman, you need to learn because I say you will learn. As for work, I do not know how you can think such a thing! You can put that idea right out of your head. I plan on turning you into an elegant young lady of whom I may be proud! And if you do well enough, I shall find you a respectable young man to marry."

Georgiana was wordless. She could scarcely believe what she had heard and felt she must be dreaming. Surely she was dreaming!

"A first lesson," came Lord Ryburn's smooth, velvet voice. "Hold your mouth closed in company."

Georgiana snapped her mouth closed. Angry and frustrated, she felt her eyes dampen. She did not know if she was more upset with herself or with Lord Ryburn—herself, surely, if she could not prevent her emotions from coming to the fore at this particular moment! She blinked, and quickly averted her eyes.

"I am sorry."

"Say 'I beg your pardon, Lord Ryburn,'" he said.

She swallowed. "I beg your pardon, L-lord Ryburn—"

"Hugh, that is quite enough! She has only just arrived. Can you not see that she is overcome by all of this?"

"You wished my assistance. I am rendering it."

"Do not be a—never mind! We shall speak more at a later time. Let us have some tea." Lady Estcott reached out and tugged the bell cord.

Georgiana had never wanted a cup of tea more than she did now, and yet when it came, she could barely swallow it. All she could think of was Lord Ryburn's obvious condescension toward her and the words with which his silky voice had wounded her.

She knew without a doubt she could never become the kind of lady who could earn the regard of someone such as Lord Ryburn. She must school herself now to learn her place. She must never again be distracted for even a moment by the attractions of a handsome gentleman who was so much above her station.

But what in the world *was* her place? What, exactly, did Lady Estcott intend for her? Oh, she had such a lot to learn!

Chapter Two

*L*ife with Lady Estcott was nothing like Georgiana had, or could have, expected. For years she had risen before dawn, stood in line to wash her face and hands in a basin of cold water, donned one of the two gowns she owned, spent the day practicing or teaching her lessons, and had gone to bed in a cold, drafty room. Georgiana had hoped for some improvement in her degree of comfort, but she still had expected to work and live the life of a servant. This was not at all the life she was to have now.

It had been all she could do not to stand like a stock and gape when she was first shown her room. She had entered ahead of the maid, glanced around, swallowed hard, and managed to maintain her dignity until she was alone—whereupon she became giddy and twirled around until she collapsed on the chaise by the fireplace. She had, however, been able to do this without uttering the slightest sound—an advantage gained from her years at Miss Silby's Academy.

This cannot truly be happening to me. She arose from the chaise to examine her quarters in more detail, and delighted in every bit of it—the ornate plaster cornice and ceiling moldings, the wood-paneled walls painted a soft golden yellow, the set of silver-backed brushes and hand mirror on the dressing table, and a delicately painted porcelain box containing pins. There was a huge wardrobe—so large that Georgiana was certain it could never be filled up—as well as a delicate writing desk of inlaid rosewood. And then there was the bed—the huge canopy bed draped in golden yellow brocade fit for a princess—or for the queen herself.

Truly, she felt she must pinch herself to see if it was all a dream, but refrained in the interest of remaining silent. It would not do for her shriek to penetrate these elegant walls! She sank down in the wing chair in happy exhaustion, waiting for the maid to return with hot water for her to refresh herself. And to think she would be brought hot water every morning—and she might even take chocolate in bed! She had this bit of information from the maid, whose information could surely be believed.

But this was only the beginning, for Lady Estcott saw her wardrobe to be in immediate need of attention, and arranged for the necessary shopping to be done as soon as possible.

This proved to be very soon, indeed. The next morning, a short while after Georgiana took breakfast with Lady Estcott and Miss Marigold Frey in the morning room, Lady Estcott's own modiste paid a visit with two servants bearing armloads of fabric. The task of "Dressing Georgiana" was staged in Lady Estcott's sitting room, where Georgiana could only observe in fascination as Lady Estcott dismissed the most beautiful fabrics in favor of others as sample upon sample was held up before Georgiana for Lady Estcott's approval.

Georgiana thought they were all beautiful. Figured muslins, shot silks, sleek satins, and lovely brocades danced before her eyes, in white, rose, azure blue, yellow, and green. A yellow-striped muslin caught her attention, but was passed over with little comment. Georgiana watched that bolt land on Lady Estcott's chaise with the others that had been discarded; then she heard a familiar male voice.

"The yellow stripe, Aunt Estcott. It would do very well as a day dress."

Georgiana snapped her head around and stared at Lord Ryburn lounging in the doorway. *Good Lord, I am standing here in my shift!* She felt her face heat violently.

Her attendant continued without pause, and lifted a swath of soft-colored blue silk in front of her.

"You may be right, Hugh. Elsie, I will have a day dress made of that muslin," said Lady Estcott.

"Yes, ma'am."

With a businesslike air, the modiste quickly retrieved the bolt.

"Lady Estcott—" Georgiana said.

"And also, if you will, hold up the rose shot silk once more. No, not that one, the other—yes, that is it."

The attendant began to withdraw the blue silk, and Georgiana snatched it and clutched it in front of her.

"Miss Marland!" cried Lady Estcott sharply. "Whatever are you doing?"

Burning with humiliation, Georgiana stared helplessly at Lady Estcott, and then glanced at Lord Ryburn. He was smiling! Or, rather, smirking. Or something in between. She didn't know exactly, except that it was clear he was amused.

"Miss Marland feels her modesty is compromised, Aunt," he said.

Lady Estcott snapped her glance back to Georgiana. "Oh, pish-tosh! Your shift covers more than most ball gowns! And I particularly want Lord Ryburn's opinion, so you will let go of that silk before you crush it completely! Now we shall have to have something made of it!"

With fear of angering Lady Estcott overpowering her modesty, Georgiana shakily released the fabric.

The attendant, brushing at the fresh wrinkles, laid it aside on the table.

"You are late," snapped Lady Estcott to her great-nephew.

"My dear Aunt, this is a great deal earlier than I generally arise in town. You are in luck."

"I wish to be luckier in the future. Do not disappoint me. Now, tell me what you think of the rose silk. Georgiana, pray stop clutching yourself like a corpse in repose. We cannot see how the fabric hangs."

Georgiana reluctantly dropped her arms to her sides as the attendant held up the silk.

It was beautiful. It was a soft shade, but deeper than a pink, with silver threads woven throughout the fabric that glittered like tiny sparks.

"Yes," Lord Ryburn said.

"I agree. This will be an evening gown, Elsie. I would like a look at the very latest styles—this gown must be absolutely à la mode."

"But of course we do not wish it to be overdone," Lord Ryburn said. "We do not wish to suggest a status to which she cannot aspire."

Lady Estcott sent her nephew a critical look. Georgiana, feeling that her humiliation was now complete, stared down at the dancing sparks of silver in the rose silk as they began to blur.

"I am completely qualified to be the judge of the styles she shall wear," Lady Estcott snapped.

"And I, as your appointed adviser, am but offering advice where I see the need."

The rose silk was swept away. Georgiana clasped her hands together and stared at her rapidly whitening knuckles.

"We are done, Elsie," said Lady Estcott. "We have immediate need for several day dresses. Can you satisfy my wishes?"

"Yes, indeed, my lady."

"Very good. Where is that maid of mine? Oh, Agnes, there you are! Take Miss Marland back to her room and make her presentable. We have much to do today."

Georgiana knew she should be grateful. She knew she should be very, very grateful . . . but as Lady Estcott's Agnes dressed her, Georgiana could not think of the lovely fabrics and the dresses they would make with the delight she had anticipated. Instead, she thought of the handsome Lord Ryburn with mockery in his eyes, the same eyes that scanned her unadorned but for her shift. It was true enough that her shift was of a heavy, serviceable material and covered her down to her toes; but a shift was a . . . well, a *shift*, and Lord Ryburn ought not to see her so! The fact that he did so with Lady Estcott's permission was very unsettling. To make it even more distressing, he seemed to lose no opportunity to remind her she was his inferior.

Georgiana began to worry about what was to

come. She had been taught modesty and manners, but not the ways of elevated persons, such as Lady Estcott and Lord Ryburn. Certainly it was no surprise that they found her ignorant, but Georgiana began to wonder if the future she faced was so splendid after all.

Of course, it all depended on whether she was lucky enough to attain the future that had been dangled before her. Then she thought of the alternative—that of a life at Miss Silby's.

She really had no choice. Whatever fate lay before her with Lady Estcott, that was the path she must take. Georgiana took a deep, settling breath as Agnes placed the last pin in her hair. She must gird herself to face the remainder of the afternoon with Lady Estcott and the intimidating Lord Ryburn.

Lord Ryburn scanned the latest *Times* in his study as he sipped his breakfast tea. Thoughts of Miss Marland intruded, however, until he lowered the paper and frowned at the tea leaves in the bottom of his cup. Thinking of Miss Marland seemed to have become part of his morning routine for the past fortnight, since the day he had attended Miss Marland's fashion consultation at his aunt's request.

He had rather enjoyed his afternoon with Miss Marland. She was clearly in awe of him, and the combination of that with her luminous beauty and her schoolgirl modesty charmed him. Her shift could not have been less revealing—he was certain she would not be able to wear it, with its high neck and long sleeves, under fashionable gowns—but she had reacted as if he had seen her wearing something *much* less concealing.

There was a sweetness about her that he liked very much.

Therein lay the danger. He could not afford to feel too charitable toward the girl. His duty was to steer his aunt clear of a disastrous association, should Miss Marland's past prove to hide some unsavory secret.

He had no personal objection to the young woman. Miss Marland was lamentably ignorant of the ways of good society, but she had been schooled in some fashion, and it was likely the school that had prevented her from developing an unsavory character. He thanked the fates for that, or he would have much greater concern for Aunt Estcott. But there were still questions to which he needed answers before he would be comfortable with his aunt's plans for Miss Marland. At the very least he needed to know more about Miss Marland's mother. His man had confirmed that Mrs. Marland had dropped out of sight several years ago, after she had discontinued supporting her daughter at Miss Silby's Academy, but Hugh was not satisfied with that.

In the meantime, he must watch Aunt Estcott. His aunt had bought more gowns for the girl than he thought necessary for her status, and she had indulged in some very expensive fabrics. With his eye for fashion, he concurred with her judgment—the gowns would do the girl justice—but he had great reservations. Miss Marland would be a pauper dressed as an heiress—a girl of common pedigree being paraded in the fashions of the most eligible daughters of the titled.

His aunt might hope for a gentleman for Miss Marland, providing she supply the inducement of a small dowry, but might such an extreme presentation of Miss Marland put off the very sort of gentleman she needed to interest, one who did not associate with the cream of society her costume would represent? And even worse, would his aunt's circle resent such a girl, dressed above her status and means?

Miss Marland now had the rudiments of a decent wardrobe in her possession, according to his aunt, who wished to show her off to him as well as discuss the next steps in the girl's preparation for her social debut. Hugh meant to speak with his aunt of his concerns when he visited this afternoon. He had delayed his decision to speak more forthrightly; it was usually best to allow Aunt Escott to proceed unquestioned for a time before giving voice to reservations. At least then she could not accuse him of rejecting her judgment out of hand.

He would still need to proceed with care. His aunt was very proud and very stubborn. Come what may, at least he would get to see the beautiful Miss Marland again . . . and to have another glimpse of her incredibly blue eyes.

Hugh set forth less than an hour later. He drew his phaeton up in front of his aunt's residence, jumped down, and tossed the reins to the footman who had come running. Without a word, he strode to the door and let himself in.

He was greeted by the distant sound of the pianoforte from the drawing room above. Whoever was playing the instrument demonstrated excellent skill—no, more than excellent skill, for the music possessed exquisite sensitivity and feeling. Somewhat enlivened, he rapidly climbed the stairs.

He found his great-aunt in the rear parlor, the room she liked to use as a second drawing room, along with the faithful Marigold. A gentleman sat with them, and all were engrossed in the music.

Miss Marland was at the pianoforte.

Lord Ryburn stopped short in surprise and watched her. Young Miss Marland wore a simple white gown, her shimmering black hair put up in such a way that glossy ringlets spilled down her shoulders. She was intent on her task, and yet there was ease in her movements. He sensed that her thoughts were completely in the music, far away from his aunt's parlor.

She played exquisitely. There was no other word to describe it. Perhaps the piece she played was not the most complicated; perhaps her technique was not the most perfect he had ever heard; but for feeling alone, for the pure eloquence of it, he was completely captivated.

His enchantment with the music immediately encompassed the musician. As certainly as he had ever understood anything, he knew that Miss Marland was not just an extraordinarily beautiful young woman, but one who was a good deal more interesting than he had supposed. The idea that she concealed such depths piqued his curiosity as nothing else could.

She finished the beautiful piece and did not look up from the keys until the gentleman who sat with Aunt Estcott called out his praise. "Excellent, my dear, excellent! Remarkable indeed."

"Is it not?" said Aunt Estcott. "Only think how exceptional her playing would be with formal instruction."

"I agree completely, and I should be honored to be her teacher."

Hugh stepped forward. "Hello, Aunt Estcott. Miss Frey. Miss Marland."

All looked at him. The gentleman rose.

"Lord Ryburn," said Aunt Estcott, "this is Mr. May, whom I am engaging to teach piano to Miss Marland. Mr. May, may I present my great-nephew, Lord Ryburn."

Hugh made the appropriate response and waited impatiently for the gentleman to leave. Once he did,

Hugh gave his full attention to Miss Marland. She was already looking at him, her blue eyes wide and expectant.

"You do have a remarkable talent," he said.

Miss Marland colored lightly. "Thank you, Lord Ryburn."

"I am very glad to hear you call it remarkable," said his aunt.

He allowed his gaze to linger on Miss Marland, fully cognizant of her unease at being the focus of his attention. She was of inferior standing, vulnerable and innocent. . . . He never toyed with such a woman, much less a favorite of his aunt's. But the devil was in it for him, for he felt the temptation. "I speak the truth. I am frank about that which I do not like, and am equally frank about that which I approve."

"His praise is infrequent," Lady Estcott informed Miss Marland, "and so you may be pleased. But I expect you already know he is a stickler for details."

"I thank you again, Lord Ryburn."

"You need only call me by name once. 'My lord' suffices thereafter in the conversation."

"Yes," said Lady Estcott, "but do not call him 'my lord' too often. It is very ill bred. That you must avoid at all costs."

Georgiana looked from Lady Estcott to Lord Ryburn and back again. Lord Ryburn stood still, watching her in that particularly intent way as she sat at the pianoforte. She sensed that Lord Ryburn intended to test her in some way, and her peace was shattered. "Thank you for your advice," she said quietly.

"Can you please tell me," said Lord Ryburn, walking slowly toward her, "how you came to play so very well?" He paused by the piano.

Georgiana moved her gaze back to the keyboard. "I enjoy music very much. There was a music room at the school, and Miss Silby, upon learning of my interest, encouraged me. She allowed me to use the pianoforte at any time to practice, and instructed me when she could."

"I am surprised that Miss Silby had the talent to instruct you so well."

"She had an interest in music herself and had fortunately been instructed when she was young."

"You were lucky to have Miss Silby."

"Yes, I know I was. I am very grateful for her tutoring."

"Miss Silby's seems to have been an exceptional institution given its modest reputation."

"Perhaps. I would not know, as I have known no other school. But Miss Silby did not encourage everyone."

"She did not?"

"I am sorry, that must sound boastful. I only meant that she would encourage an interest where she saw it. For me, she encouraged my music."

"I should like to hear another piece. Can you oblige me?"

Georgiana stared at the keys. She felt nervous, which never happened when she was playing, and she knew that Lord Ryburn was the cause. He was so tall, stately, and handsome, and he stood so near that she could smell a softly sweet scent from him that was both exotic and intoxicating.

Her fingers found the keys. Drawing a breath, she began a sweet Haydn minuet. For the briefest moment her fingers seemed clumsy, but then they found their speed and grace. Once she let her heart go free, the notes came alive like the song of a golden bird. She was not aware of time passing—she never was while she played. And when her hands stilled at last, she sat for a moment in a kind of surprising void as the world slowly returned to her.

She heard Lord Ryburn's intake of breath. "Lovely," he said softly.

She glanced up at him and met his eyes, so intently golden, fixed on her own. Her heart fluttered. "Thank you, Lo-my lord."

A slow smile crooked up the corners of his mouth. "You are very welcome, Miss Marland."

If the heavens swallow me up this very moment and dress me in white and crown me in gold, it could not feel like this. It cannot feel like this!

Georgiana could not tear her gaze away. And while she sat thus, her hands yet poised on the keys, he raised his hand and gently, gently lifted a curl from her cheek and tucked it back behind her shoulder.

Her heart, fluttering in indecision, burst into flame.

"Hugh," came Lady Estcott's querulous voice, "do not set about confusing Miss Marland. She is to learn what to expect in polite society, not to indulge liberties!"

"I am teaching her what to expect, Aunt," he said gently. "Miss Marland, you are to respond to such forwardness thus. Say 'Sir!' in a sharp and contemptuous voice, then step back."

Georgiana swallowed. "But I am seated," she said.

"Then move away—but move away you must."

Georgiana continued to stare at him, feeling the touch of his fingertip again on her cheek. Then, hesitantly, she leaned away from him.

"You forgot to address me. Say 'Sir!' very loudly." He extended his reach and again captured a ringlet between his fingers.

"Sir!" She leaned even more to evade his touch, and was now near to tumbling from her chair.

"My dear Miss Marland, I barely heard you. And you must look the part of a highly outraged lady. Your expression resembles that of a kicked spaniel."

"That is enough, Hugh!" exclaimed Lady Estcott. "You do wear on my nerves. Let the poor girl alone."

"Perhaps this lesson is a bit advanced for you," he said, and the amused smile was back on his lips.

"Please—before you take a tumble—permit me to assist."

He cupped her shoulders and shifted her upright in her chair. His touch was gone before she could comprehend what had happened, but the sensation of his hands on her shoulders remained until Lady Estcott's voice intruded.

"Miss Marland, can you please go and find Mrs. Mitchell for me? Ask any of the footmen for her whereabouts. Go along!"

Georgiana rose from her chair by the pianoforte and crossed the room toward the door, confused by Lady Estcott's strange request for the housekeeper. She stepped out just as Lady Estcott spoke once more.

"Come here, Hugh. I mean to have a word with you."

"Do not play the innocent with me, Hugh Edmund Fitzadam! You are not to flirt with Miss Marland. I may be old, but I am not blind, and I have every wit I ever possessed, sharpened to a fine point!"

Hugh wisely succumbed. Whenever his aunt used his given name, she was seriously annoyed. Besides, he was more than a little provoked with himself. He *was* guilty of teasing Miss Marland; he did not know where his head had been.

"I am sorry, Aunt Estcott. Forgive me?"

"Do not look at me so. I am not so forgiving as your young ladies—if they may be called *ladies*."

"But I mean it sincerely. Yes, I did flirt with her. But truthfully, she must learn how to defend herself from such behavior. You must realize how extraordinarily beautiful she is."

"Again, Hugh, I am perfectly cognizant of her appearance." She paused and her face softened. "She *is* beautiful, is she not?"

"Yes. She is." Hugh gazed at Lady Estcott, who sat with him in the now private drawing room. A brightness had appeared in her shrewd, old eyes, and he wondered what she was planning.

"I do believe she is more beautiful than Arietta ever was."

"Arietta? Who is Arietta?"

"Oh, never mind." She waved her hand dismissively. "I mean to say that I believe she is the most beautiful girl of the season."

Hugh said nothing. The direction of his aunt's thoughts bothered him, but he dared not mortify her before she finished speaking.

"All she needs is a bit of polish and a few lessons. Of course, she does need to learn to dance. She has informed me that she does not dance a step. Can you imagine! What sort of school can that Miss Silby's be?

"As I said, it is not the best sort of—"

"*You* shall instruct her!"

Openmouthed, Hugh found himself the target of his aunt's long, extended, beringed finger. "I? Instruct her to—?"

"Dance, of course! You are exquisite on the dance floor, Hugh, as well you know. I have always said so. You shall teach Miss Marland."

"But I—"

"You agreed to help, did you not?"

"Yes."

"Then you shall instruct Miss Marland in dancing. *And . . .* you shall *not* flirt with her. Is that understood?"

Hugh sighed. "I am at your service."

Chapter Three

*L*ord Ryburn touched his sleek chestnut with his whip and directed his phaeton to pass the slow-moving farmer's wagon. The horse, not happy with the noise and clatter of the London street and still less happy with the wagonload of alarmed chickens in front of him, decided to display his protest by attempting to rear. The caged birds exploded into a mass of flapping wings, Lord Ryburn cursed, and the street urchins cried out their delight at the sight of a "foine gentl'mun" struggling with his horse, a sight made even more delightful by a Royal Mail coach bearing down upon him.

Lord Ryburn regained control, skirted the cartload of fowl with an inch to spare, and regained his course—with a detestable splatter of mud on his beige pantaloons, which had somehow discovered the gap in his overcoat.

Lord Ryburn was out of sorts.

Lord Ryburn was out of sorts because lately things were not going the usual way of "Lucky Hughie." No, he had not lost at cards; in any event, he was not much of a gambler. But in the space of a fortnight he had had to do the pretty to the Honorable Miss Hartley and her mother and had agreed to school this Miss Marland in dancing! What was he reduced to then, a tame beau? A *dancing-master*? And what sort of dancing-master would lower himself to instruct a young miss of no particular family?

At least she is attractive. Attractive? She is devilish out of the ordinary. But a vestal virgin might as well tempt me as Miss Marland!

He had, in fact, come to the conclusion that Miss Marland was the most beautiful young woman he had ever encountered. The irony of the situation was not lost on him. "Lucky Hughie," wealthy, handsome, and heir to an earldom, had his choice of mistresses and potential brides alike, the fact that he was not eager to marry notwithstanding. But Miss Marland was neither fish nor fowl—she was completely inedible. She was the unknown Captain Marland's daughter, quite ineligible, but supposedly of good character—so quite unavailable to any proposal other than one of marriage.

He would, however, discover if she was of good character or not. Upon that he was now fully resolved. He dared not trust the appearance of innocence when so much was at stake. He was *not* about to allow his great-aunt to be taken in! His aunt might interfere with him excessively, but he loved her, and he would protect her even if it meant stopping her from presenting Miss Marland. He would save his aunt from the humiliation of scandal whether she liked it or not!

Hugh arrived at his aunt's town house with his heart steeled against the temptation of Miss Marland's blue eyes.

Were they blue? No, not merely blue. They contained a tinge of violet.

Hugh tossed the reins to his tiger, mounted the steps in a leap, and opened the door in the face of his aunt's startled butler.

"My lord!" the butler said.

Wordlessly, Hugh gave him his hat and set forth for the stairs. He thought the ladies would be in the great parlor where they could make use of the pianoforte; as he reached the first landing, he heard the sound of a waltz being played.

It was not Miss Marland at the keys this time. It was Miss Frey. Hugh paused in the open doorway to observe.

Miss Marland stood in the center of the room, listening to Aunt Estcott instruct her in the steps. Miss Marland looked nonplussed.

"You must now take your partner's hand," his aunt was saying, "and go round in a circle. No, not that way—rather as though you are changing places. Cross and stand where he was standing."

Hugh watched with a smile tugging on his lips. Poor Miss Marland! After recovering from her mistake, she crossed the imaginary aisle and stood where her make-believe partner had been standing.

"Oh, never mind, Miss Marland! Marigold, please stop playing. We must start afresh!"

At that moment his aunt caught a glimpse of him in the doorway, and his solitary amusement was over.

"Hugh! Do not stand there. We are in need of a partner for Miss Marland."

"I am here to supply myself, as commanded," he said, and walked slowly into the room. As he approached he caught Miss Marland's eye and carefully schooled his expression to one of indifference. At the same time, he reined in his troublesome liking for her—it seemed to overcome him like a draft of strong spirits whenever he so much as saw her. He would do what he must, and any attraction to the young lady was most certainly not a good thing. "Miss Marland, is there not a dance of which you know the steps?"

Miss Marland blushed. She looked absolutely lovely today, he thought. She wore a yellow figured muslin, and her hair was in a most flattering arrangement of coils and ringlets.

"We practiced the minuet at the academy." She paused and moistened her lips. "And once, a gavotte, but Miss Silby did not feel it was of benefit to young ladies."

"We have covered the basic movements, but there is little more we can do without you," Aunt Estcott said to him. "Miss Marland needs to practice."

Hugh gazed at Miss Marland. She looked so vulnerable, and so hopeful, that he found it hard to keep his heart hardened against her. He would teach her to dance, but he would not rest until he knew everything there was to know about Miss Marland, even if it meant her ruin.

"Miss Frey, pray begin once more," his aunt commanded.

He bowed as the music started, and Georgiana curtsied. Then he stepped forward and reached out for her hand, and they began the dance.

He learned with surprise that Miss Marland was a natural. Her movements were light and graceful, and she recovered easily when she did not anticipate the step. Her face flushed a delicate pink with the exercise, and when he glimpsed her lovely blue eyes, they gazed back with a captivating brilliance.

"You do very well," he said at last.

"You are an excellent teacher, sir."

"I believe we must add dancing to your list of talents."

She did not answer until they completed the next movement. "You are kind. My list of talents is very brief."

"Ah, but you must never confess this. Always behave as though you have a great many talents. To confess a shortcoming is a faux pas in itself."

"Is it not deceiving to act so? And is not deceit a bad thing?"

"In good society, deceit can be a very *good* thing."

Here she began to turn in the wrong direction.

"Left, please," he said.

She quickly recovered, and they completed the dance without speaking.

"Excellent!" said Aunt Estcott. "I am very pleased. You learn very quickly, my dear."

"Thank you, ma'am."

Hugh bowed to Miss Marland; she curtsied in return, and he turned to face his aunt. "Are we finished, then?"

"Yes, I think we have done enough dancing for today. I mean to take Miss Marland out for a drive at Hyde Park. I hope you will accompany us."

Hugh drew a breath. He was not in favor of this, particularly not to lending his face to Miss Marland's first public appearance. However, there seemed to be no avoiding it, and so he consented.

"Very well. But I shall ride alongside."

"But of course. I want Miss Marland to be seen, and I would like you to provide your support—

unless you are seeing Miss Hartley this afternoon. You have not yet proposed marriage to her?"

"No, indeed I have not."

"I am expecting news in that quarter. I hope I shall not wait long for it."

"You shall not." Hugh looked back at Miss Marland then, not at all willing to pursue this particular conversation with his aunt. Truth be told, he was in no great hurry to secure Miss Hartley. "Miss Marland is more interested in the afternoon drive, I am sure. Is that not so, Miss Marland?"

He turned back to his aunt without awaiting an answer. "I shall be here at four o'clock exactly, and we shall be off."

"Very well, Hugh. I am counting on it."

It had only been a practice dance, but when Lord Ryburn stepped forward and reached for her hand, Georgiana had felt a warm fluttering in her breast. She realized, with quiet surprise, that she held this difficult gentleman in considerable regard. She was beneath him, and yet . . . and yet the touch of his hand was warm and real. For just that moment, he did not seem unreachable at all.

It was a foolish thought, of course, but she could enjoy the playacting. While Lord Ryburn guided her through the dance, she could pretend it was real. She could pretend the drawing room was decorated with flowers, that it glowed with the light of a hundred candles or more, and that the air was scented with the exotic perfumes of the guests. Miss Frey's pedantic performance at the pianoforte became the music of a string quartet, and Lord Ryburn's light touch became not merely practiced, but one of affection.

And I am become a fine lady. Ha.

She stifled a laugh and smiled instead. He smiled back. Then he made that remark: "*In good society, deceit can be a very good thing.*"

It would be wise to remember that they are different than you are, she thought. *As the dance is an act, so is his smile.*

Now, she knew something of even more consequence. There was a Miss Hartley. Who was Miss Hartley? But it did not matter who she was, or whether she was beautiful or horse-faced. She was someone Lady Estcott approved of as his future wife.

Thoughts of Miss Hartley and her imagined qualities haunted Georgiana during the brief ride in Lady Estcott's carriage to the Hyde Park entrance. She gazed out, hardly knowing what she was seeing until they turned into the gates. The park was quite filled with riders and carriages, but it was Lord Ryburn who caught her eye as he came riding up from behind.

He reined back his horse and rode up to the window. "I shall take a turn about the park. I shall be back shortly."

His aunt nodded. "Very well."

Lord Ryburn was off, and the ladies' carriage continued at a sedate pace, blending in with the line of vehicles in front of them.

"Everyone who is anyone may be seen here," Lady Estcott said. "That is why one comes, to see and be seen. And one expects what one does to be reported upon, so it is very important how you conduct yourself, and with whom."

"I understand."

Privately, she did not see how she could fall into error. She was reserved by nature, and those she observed through her window were either talking or quietly observing from their carriages, as she was. Then there were the riders on horseback, who rode with a stylish quietude when they were not in conversation. There were also those who walked, and she gazed at them with some longing. She would much rather take a turn on foot in this lovely park, but that must await Lady Estcott's pleasure.

But the dress! The ladies were elegant in the most fashionable attire, and it made her give a concerned glance at her own costume, although it was the most stunning she had ever possessed. It had only been delivered yesterday—a white cambric dress with delicate ovals of lacework all over it, and a blue satin spencer over that. She wore a hat to match, as well— a small, silk creation decorated with violets. She had thrilled at her reflection in the looking glass, but in the midst of the best of the *ton*, she felt more the insignificant flower wilting in the sun. In the next moment she came to an uncomfortable realization about herself. *I am become vain.* Georgiana leaned back against the soft cushions of the coach, drawing her eyes away from the scene of the park. *I am Georgiana Marland, daughter of a naval officer. I had best preserve my wits, for they are my most precious possession. I must not be seduced by all of this.*

"Miss Marland, I must use your eyes. Look at the carriage across the way—the one with the disagreeable old woman who is chatting with the gentleman on the gray horse. I must know who is in the carriage with her."

"I cannot see well from this side, ma'am."

"Drat. I *must* see who it is." Lady Estcott picked up her cane and rapped the roof with surprising force.

"Coachman! Turn back. Stay closer to the middle!"

"Yes, mum."

The coach turned, and Georgiana now had a better view of the riders and equipages in the center of the park.

"There!" said Lady Estcott. "You can observe the carriage now. Try to see the lady's companion. Do not try to call my attention, for I shall not look."

Lady Estcott was looking in the opposite direction with her chin held high. Georgiana turned back to her window.

The "disagreeable old woman" was a petite, sharp-faced lady of advanced years, dressed very fashionably, and completely in black. She chatted with considerable eagerness with the gentleman, who nodded and smiled, but when the young woman beside the older lady leaned forward, his smile grew.

Georgiana caught a glimpse of blond curls framing a pert, elfin face before the gentleman leaned down so far as to obscure her view.

"Well?" queried Lady Estcott.

"It is a young woman. She is dressed very fine, I think. She is wearing a very fashionable bonnet."

"Hm. Then she is not a companion. What else did you see?"

"She is blond. Quite pretty."

"Pretty? Do not be kind. Tell me exactly what she looks like."

"I should say she has an interesting face. She has a delicate look . . . a small chin and large eyes . . . a sweet expression. I think she is *very* pretty."

Lady Estcott did not seem pleased. "I think you did not see her well at all."

"I did not, I am afraid—"

"Sir Goodrich!" Suddenly Lady Estcott leaned forward and waved out of her window. "Sir Goodrich, a word, if you please!"

It was the gentleman on the gray horse. He saw Lady Estcott's summons and turned his horse.

"How do you do, Lady Estcott?" He smiled and tipped his hat. He was a middle-aged gentleman of no particular appearance. Georgiana thought him nothing out of the way; but clearly he was acquainted with Lady Estcott, so he was *someone*. "How may I serve you?"

"I am very well, as you can see. I feel younger every day. I have a young cousin staying with me now, and I am sponsoring her this season. Miss Marland, this is a longtime friend, Sir Goodrich. Sir Goodrich, Miss Marland, my cousin."

"How do you do, Miss Marland." He leaned down further to peer across the carriage at her, and his eyes warmed. "I am *very* pleased to meet you!"

"How do you do."

Lady Estcott leaned forward again, ending the interchange between Georgiana and Sir Goodrich. "*Now* I should like to know who is the young woman with Lady Etherington."

"Ah. So you only wanted me for information." His voice was cheerfully amused. "Why, it is her granddaughter, Miss Etherington. Lady Etherington is presenting her this season. Her mother is sickly, as I understand it."

"Her granddaughter? Then she is Lord Etherington's daughter or Mr. Charles's daughter?

"She is the daughter of her eldest son, Lord Etherington. She was very specific on that point with me."

"Yes, I am sure Arietta *would* be. She must be very disappointed that the girl is merely *pretty*. I did not get a good look at her, though. Do you agree?"

"Pretty? Lady Estcott, I do believe you are fishing!" He laughed lightly. "Very well, I shall give you my opinion. Miss Etherington is more than pretty—she is likely to be the toast of the season. So you may rest assured that Lady Etherington is not disappointed at all."

"I shall rest however I please, Sir Goodrich. Be off with you now!"

He laughed and rode away.

Lady Estcott rapped the roof. "Home!" she snapped.

She said nothing on the short return to the town house, and had Georgiana wished to express a thought, or ask a question, she would not have attempted it. Lady Estcott's dark mood warned against it. Georgiana felt discomfort at having left Lord Ryburn with no leave-taking, and although she suspected that he would go on very well without the courtesy of a good-bye, she was surprised that Lady Estcott seemed not to think of him at all.

Then, as the carriage came to a stop in front of her residence, Lady Estcott broke her silence.

"I simply will not allow it!" she announced. "Arietta will not have it all. Not this time. I shall win, or die trying!"

Chapter Four

By and by Hugh noted the absence of his aunt's coach, and began to wonder about it. Knowing his aunt, she had been annoyed at something or other and had driven home in a huff, but he could not help but ponder what it was. Could her wonderful Miss Marland have committed some serious faux pas? He rather thought not, for the girl was not so gauche as that, but he supposed she might have committed some minor offense. Or perhaps his aunt had felt faint or had the ache in her hip again.

Hugh finished his visit with an old acquaintance and completed a leisurely tour of the park while scanning for friends, familiar faces, and becoming young damsels. One young lady in particular caught his eye—a striking, young, flaxen-haired creature riding in a coach alongside her rather fierce looking dragon. The old lady did stare at him, though, as if trying to place him; it appeared she could not, for she did not have him summoned.

Hugh rode homeward at last, feeling pleasantly relieved at not having to do his aunt's bidding for the remainder of the day, as much as he would have liked to enjoy Miss Marland's pretty face a bit longer. He thought he would eat at his club tonight; it would be pleasant to relax this evening. But when he reached his town house, his butler met him with a note.

Hugh observed his aunt's hand and opened the note in the entry. He felt mildly irritated at yet another demand from her:

> *Come at once. There is a matter of importance I must discuss with you. E.E.*

"Bother," Hugh grumbled. He passed the note back to his butler. "Please send the reply that I will come. But first, I must change my shirt."

"Yes, sir."

"Do not include the matter of my shirt."

"Certainly not, sir."

Hugh sprinted up the stairs and was stripped to the waist and splashing his face before his valet entered the room.

"Sir?"

"A clean shirt."

"Immediately, sir."

"I am going to Lady Estcott's. I shall likely dine out and return late. No need to wait up for me."

Within the hour he was on his way to his aunt's. He estimated that she had written as soon as she had returned home, and since he had not hurried his own return, she would have been stewing about whatever it was for some time. He hoped she was reasonable.

He rode up to her door, passed his reins to her footman, and met her attorney, Mr. Rodney, coming down her steps as he went up.

"Good day."

"Good day, sir." Mr. Rodney looked away quickly, and Hugh recognized his guilty expression. This was not good.

He found his aunt in her back parlor, sitting at the little library table with a paper before her. She looked up with an expression of irritation on her face.

"Hugh, I thought you would never arrive! It is a lucky thing that I was not in my death throes."

"If you were, dear Aunt, you should have compelled the fates to wait for me."

"Sit down and do not be pert. I have an important matter to discuss."

Hugh took a seat opposite his aunt and caught a glimpse of his reflection in the polished brass candelabrum. It made his chin appear enormous.

"You wished to consult with me?" he asked.

"It is rather late for that, but yes. I have already made up my mind."

"On what matter?"

"The matter of Miss Marland." She paused and raised her eyebrows, conveying an attitude of great significance.

"Well?" His stomach knotted.

"I have given this considerable thought. She could be the belle of the season, Hugh. She is a smart girl. She is family, so I need not go to great lengths to explain her. It all seems so clear to me now. It is almost as if it were—ordained."

"It is an entertaining thought, but of course it cannot be so."

"Cannot be? And why not?" Aunt Estcott straightened in her chair and sent her great-nephew a haughty look. He guessed that look had shattered hearts once upon a time when his aunt had been a great beauty. It still caused considerable trepidation. "She has the connection to the family. She only lacks a respectable fortune. And I, dear Hugh, have the fortune!"

Hugh gaped at her. "You cannot—"

"Do you still believe you may tell me what I *cannot do*?"

"No—"

"I have no child. No heirs save you and your father that I would consider, and neither of you needs my help. Miss Marland does. If she stood to inherit my fortune, she could be anything I wish! I shall see about Almack's immediately. And her come-out ball simply must be the event of the season!"

"Aunt . . . " He was wordless. Possibly, he could persuade her to change her mind; he hoped that he could. But at the moment, his wits were useless.

"It is settled. This is what you get for not coming to me immediately, Hugh. I had to resolve this at all speed, and I have!"

"It hardly needed to be decided today."

"Of course it did. I need to secure the very best date for her ball before it is overtaken by too many other engagements. Few will attempt to compete with me, but I must be first with the invitations! It shall be a crush, for everyone will be curious. *That* will put a curl in Arietta's nose!"

Hugh still did not know who Arietta was, and at the moment he did not care in the least. "You must not rush this, Aunt. We must be very sure that Miss Marland is—is deserving of your recognition. We still do not know what happened to her mother, or if there are any undesirable relations on her maternal side. You *must* allot time for us to discover everything we need to know!"

"Have you not already been prodding into her past?" His aunt's stare pierced him like a blade. "I know you, Hugh, so do not think I am unaware of your actions. You have had time enough to learn anything of a shocking nature. I am certain of that."

"I have not had nearly time enough. Her mother has not been located."

"Then she cannot be found. If that is the case, no one else will find her, either, and we may as well accept it. Miss Marland believes she is dead, and that suffices."

"She *said* her mother is dead. She did not say she *believes* her mother is dead. There is a difference. She claims her mother is dead, but she cannot substantiate it, and therefore she is guilty of telling an untruth. For that reason, I cannot rest until I know the fact of the matter!"

"Very well, Hugh, do not rest. But *I* shall continue with my plans, so be prepared to conceal all the unsavory particulars you expect to find!"

Hugh left in some temper, which he hoped he had hidden from his aunt. He did not see Miss Marland. She was likely congratulating herself for an excellent coup, wherever she was! Hugh mounted his horse, and instead of riding to James Street and his club, he turned toward the outskirts of town where his father's London home lay. Hugh was determined to bend his sire's ear that evening.

Hopefully, his father was not visiting his current mistress or attending the soirée of one of his married lady loves. His father, whose indifference toward business matters seemed to be balanced by a good deal of luck, was not Hugh's choice as adviser—but in this matter he had no alternative.

Should Aunt Estcott plunge precipitately into her plans and some devastating secret about Miss Marland then come to light, the entire family would be tarnished. Hugh would lose Miss Hartley, who might well be his best choice as bride. Even his father would be touched by the scandal. His sire would hate to see a decrease in invitations to the homes of his favorite hostesses.

Perhaps this time Lord Wyndgrave would be sufficiently concerned to speak with Aunt Estcott and hopefully convince her to allow a more thorough investigation of Miss Marland before she thrust the girl upon the *ton*.

Hugh strode up the steps of his father's house and across the small Italianate portico, and was immediately admitted into the entrance hall. It was much too fussy for Hugh's taste, and he quickly bypassed the marble cherubs, the rococo plasterwork with the excess of gold leaf, and the mirrors, and mounted the stairs. He found his father in his dressing room, relaxing on a chaise in his robe and sipping a glass of wine with his eyes closed. One hand hung down, lazily fondling his favorite greyhound, which lay loyally at his side.

The hound's eyes opened wide and focused warily on Hugh. Its slender gray body tensed.

"Hugh, you must not visit me in one of your states. You frighten my bitch."

If his father's eyes had as much as cracked open, Hugh had not seen it. He was used to his father's unusual perception, however, and seated himself in a nearby chair to regard his father purposefully.

At a glance, one might think that Lord Wyndgrave was a soft, self-indulgent man who rarely stirred himself to any strenuous action. Hugh knew, however, that in an instant his father could have sword in hand and disembowel a foe. At three-and-fifty, Lord Wyndgrave was very fit; he was extremely fond of fencing, and had introduced Hugh to the sport when Hugh was but a boy.

It bothered Hugh more than a little that he and his father were so very similar. Both were tall, well-formed, and adept at physical sport. Both bore the same striking Wyndgrave face. They had the same well-set shoulders and the same head of wavy blond hair, although Lord Wyndgrave's was liberally streaked with gray. But Lord Wyndgrave roused himself to defend family and honor only when danger was imminent. He was like a sleeping cat, completely relaxed one instant, and at the throat of his enemy the next—usually at the last possible moment.

Hugh preferred a more pragmatic approach. He felt that potential problems should be prevented.

"What is the matter today, my boy?" Lord Wyndgrave asked. He took another sip of wine. His eyes remained closed.

"I wish to discuss a matter of importance concerning our Aunt Estcott. She has made a very imprudent decision."

Lord Wyndgrave shrugged his brows. "She is five-and-seventy if she is a day. If you hope to change her, you may as well attempt to change a dead horse into a live one. It would be simpler."

"A live horse will not save the family from ruin."

"Ah! You are getting to the point now, are you?"

"She has taken in a young woman whom no one knows anything about, and plans to make her her heiress!"

Lord Wyndgrave's eyes cracked open. "Is that so? Well, God bless the old girl. She had been getting rather lifeless of late."

"Damme, Father, she plans to present this girl to the cream of society! She is after vouchers to Almack's, for the Lord's sake!"

"Well, one must not fuss over that. Stands to reason she will not get them if the girl don't qualify."

"That will not stop her from presenting her to the very first circles, and making a damnable fool of herself! She is spending a small fortune on the girl's gowns, and she has even pressed *me* into teaching her to dance!"

"Bless me, Son, but she plans to match you up with her! How amusing! I thought she intended you to marry Miss—er, that other young lady."

"I am not going to marry this chit, only school her. And it certainly is not amusing!"

Hugh stood and stalked to the broad French windows of his father's study and stared out at the neat formal garden. It gave him a moment to rein in his impatience. "Do you recall a Captain Marland?" he asked.

"Marland? No. Cannot say that I do."

"Well, he was this girl's father. He is some distant connection of Aunt Estcott's family—dead, of course—and she has taken this girl in on the strength of that alone. Of course, the girl has an angel's face. That is likely what has sealed the thing."

Lord Wyndgrave, who had sat comfortably sipping wine during his son's tirade, seemed to take an interest here. "An angel's face? And you find yourself inconvenienced? This is not like you, Hugh. Not like you at all."

Hugh turned around and sent his sire a quelling look, which was as ineffectual when used on his father as it was on his great-aunt Estcott.

"That is neither here nor there. Aunt Estcott is absolutely set upon leaving this girl her entire fortune and finding her a husband from the very first circles! And here we have a father who was next to nobody, and a mother who cannot even be found! Does that make no impression upon you at all? This is not about my pleasure or lack of it. It is about Aunt Estcott!"

Lord Wyndgrave remained infuriatingly unmoved. "I do not need her money. A disappointment, perhaps . . . but one should not count upon such things. Neither should you. You shall give yourself an apoplectic attack and die—and the last I knew, you had no heir."

Hugh threw up his arms. "I do wish you would stop being droll, sir! We cannot be certain of this girl's character. Aunt Estcott is confident that Miss Marland is as pure and good as her face, based solely on the girl's upbringing at a third rate young ladies' academy. And even if the girl is well behaved and trustworthy, what if some hidden scandal is attached to her or her missing family?"

Lord Wyndgrave raised his eyebrows and made an expression that was both incredulous and dismissive. "Hugh, there is more than a little of your mother in you, after all. Aunt Estcott knows what she is about. I suggest you let her do as she likes. You are fretting and poking about looking for trouble, and all to no purpose."

"It is not to no purpose. This could impact all of us. Recall that Aunt Estcott expects me to marry an icon of society in the midst of it! It is incomprehensible!"

Hugh slapped his hand against the side of the bookcase. The greyhound leapt up and shot under the desk.

Lord Wyndgrave gave a slight shrug. "My dear

Son, life is to enjoy. At the moment, you are making me enjoy mine rather less. I should like to taste this very fine wine I have here, and you should be considering how best to make use of your lucky proximity to this very beautiful young woman."

"You forget that I am courting Miss Hartley."

"All the more reason, my boy. All the more reason."

And so that was how Hugh's visit with his father ended. Lord Wyndgrave, a rogue with the ladies in his day—and sometimes still when the opportunity presented itself—had no better advice to his son than to seize the chance to flirt. Hugh was thoroughly disgruntled. As much as Hugh enjoyed the ladies, he felt there was a time for serious thought; his father never did. No, he and his father were not the least bit alike. They were not alike at all!

Chapter Five

As his father would be of no help, Hugh decided that his only choice was to see what he could discover on his own about Mrs. Marland. His agent, unfortunately, had come up with little. He had interviewed Miss Silby at the academy, but an old address was the only result.

Subsequently, Lord Ryburn decided to visit the school himself. It was located some little distance from his town house, in a respectable section of the city, but not overly so; it was a bit too far south, and too close to the Thames for the area to be favored, but well enough for a middle-class establishment. Lord Ryburn drew up in front of the unpretentious old building, distinguished from its neighbors primarily by a larger wood door and the hanging sign proclaiming it to be Miss Silby's Academy for Young Ladies.

Lord Ryburn was admitted into the entrance hall by an old woman in a cap who appeared to be the housekeeper. She begged him to follow her and tottered away, leading him to a door that opened into a small room.

"A gentlemun t' see you, mum, a Lord Ryburn, he says."

With that introduction, Hugh stepped into the office of Miss Silby, proprietress.

Miss Silby was a slim woman, dressed in black, her dark hair put up under a white cap. She was seated behind a wood writing desk, quill in hand when he entered. Upon seeing him, she laid it down, rose, and gave him a brief curtsy. Then she gazed at him with remarkably clear gray eyes.

"Please be seated, your lordship, and tell me your business." She resituated herself, and he sat opposite her in the small straight-backed chair provided for visitors.

He could not help but notice the simplicity of the furnishings. There were bookshelves against one wall and two small portraits, one of an older gentleman and one of a lady, hung behind her. On a small table in the corner were a teapot, a cup, and a small glass holding a handful of violets. That was all.

"I am in search of information about a Mrs. Marland, the mother of a Miss Marland who has recently taken up residence in my aunt's household."

"I see. I believe a gentleman who represented your

lordship came here on that same quest very lately. I provided him with the last address we have for Mrs. Marland. I am afraid I can do no more for you."

"Perhaps not. But if I may ask a few questions?"

"Of course."

"How did it come about that you lost contact with Mrs. Marland?"

Miss Silby raised her dark brows. "She discontinued payment for her daughter's education. Under the circumstances, no further correspondence ensued. We were able to employ Miss Marland, as you know, and she was a teacher in this school until your aunt desired her."

"Did you know anything of Mrs. Marland's circumstances at the time?"

"No more than what she wrote to us. She stated she was unable to continue payment. I do hope you are not questioning Miss Marland's reputation, your lordship. She was a very good teacher and a hard worker. We never had the least reason to doubt her trustworthiness or her ability."

"No, I am not. But in her present circumstances, it is best that we discover all we can about her family. My aunt is quite fond of her."

Miss Silby seemed slightly relieved. "That is good, for we are in no position to take her back. Another girl has taken her place. I wish to point out to you, sir, that we did provide a reference to Lady Estcott. Nothing more was requested."

"I understand. But if there is anything more you can think of now—any additional information about Mrs. Marland—it could be extremely useful."

Miss Silby hesitated a moment, then opened a drawer in her desk and withdrew a folded piece of paper. "Perhaps you would like to see this. It is Mrs. Marland's last letter to me."

Hugh reached out and took the paper, then unfolded it. It was short, and written in a woman's ornate hand:

> *Dear Miss Silby,*
> *I am writing sadly to inform you that I can no longer pay the way of my daughter at your school. She has turned sixteen, and I know she has excelled in her studies. I hope and pray you may engage her as one of your teachers so that she may stay on and earn her way.*
> *I shall be at this address for one more fortnight, if you will be so kind as to write me your answer. If you can provide a position for my daughter, please give her the letter I have enclosed to her.*
> *Sincerely, Mrs. G. Marland*

When Hugh finished reading the note, he handed it back to Miss Silby. "That is all?"

"Yes. She never contacted us again."

"You have no idea to what kind of situation she might have gone?"

Miss Silby gave him that quizzical lift of her brows

again. "I should have no idea." She paused. "I can only tell you, Lord Ryburn, that she was a very beautiful woman, for whatever that may be worth. I do believe she has found something."

Hugh rose and made his good-bye, and shortly thereafter stepped from the entrance hall onto the street. He saw his phaeton approaching, his tiger at the reins, and had just paused to wait when a quiet voice made him turn.

A thin-faced woman had just stepped through the doorway of Miss Silby's. Glancing quickly behind her, she silently closed the door and turned to him.

"I know something, if it is worth anything to you," she whispered.

Hugh gazed down at her sharp, dark eyes and felt an instant dislike for the woman. Liking her was not important, however; obtaining information was. He withdrew a coin. "Here is a crown."

"It is perhaps worth more than that t'you, your lordship?"

"Two, then."

"Very well." She held out a thin hand, and he dropped the coins into it. She tucked them quickly into the pocket of her dress.

"I saw Mrs. Marland just last week," she said. "She didn't see me. She drove up very slowly in a fine carriage with a gentleman, and looked out the window."

"What gentleman?"

"I do not know, but a fine gentleman, to be sure. He was an older, distinguished sort of man."

"And then what did she do?"

"That was all. She just looked out, kind of lonesomelike, and they kept on going."

It was not much for two crown, but it was apparently all he was going to get. Hugh walked to his phaeton, wondering what to think of this new information and how much he needed to worry about it.

Georgiana had been nearly a month at Lady Estcott's Park Lane residence. In the parks, the trees had exploded into full leaf, the daffodils were in bloom, and people abounded—ladies and gentlemen, nurses and infants, young bucks and pretty maids.

At first she was overwhelmed by her new existence. There seemed to be much more that she did not know than she did, so she said little, listened and observed—all the while dressed in gowns too pretty to sit down in!

She at last acknowledged the truth of it. It was as wearying as her old life at Miss Silby's Academy, and she truly could not say that she was any happier. The specter of failure lurked relentlessly, so she might claim no peace in her new situation. Perhaps worst of all was the sometimes charming, sometimes unfeeling Lord Ryburn, keeping her on her toes and off-balance all at once, so she never understood how he thought of her. One would think a kindness cost him a small fortune!

Perhaps the stars were falling from her eyes, for she was beginning to lose her awe of him. She saw him less as a lord of great stature and more as a man like any other—a man who was not perfect. And yet . . . she was not precisely angry with him. There were times she saw an emotion in his eyes, just before it was quickly hidden, that told her something about Lord Ryburn that she knew he would not willingly reveal. It was something almost desperate . . . or perhaps a certain longing. . . . Whether acknowledged or denied, it was locked away from sight.

She sighed, looked back at the volume of poetry she held, and then laid it aside. She had taken the opportunity to sit in her own room in blessed privacy, for Lady Escott was not well today and had cancelled their plans. Although she was concerned for Lady Escott, she was not sorry to be denied company this morning or an outing this afternoon. There would be no gown fittings or lessons on how to walk, curtsy, greet her betters, or converse.

At Miss Silby's she would not have had this luxury, but yet there was a degree of freedom there that she did not have here. When she taught her girls their lessons, she had a modicum of control over what she said or did not say. When she practiced the pianoforte at Miss Silby's, it had been thankfully without an audience. On those occasions when she was allowed out to go on an errand, she had been able to walk alone, or with one of the older girls, and felt quite independent. Finally, she was thought to know how to act, how to speak, and how to feel— and she had truly believed she knew all the things that a young gentlewoman should know—but here, all that was changed.

And yet, for the little freedoms she had had, Miss Silby's had been another prison in its own way.

Georgiana lay back on her chaise and stared at her plasterwork ceiling. The dips and swirls, the hills and valleys seemed somehow an allegory of her life. Whenever she felt safe, an obstacle presented itself; when happiness beckoned, her path curved away.

She missed her father, but now the pang in her heart was old and softened, and he was harder and harder to remember. He had been happy and loud, his big hands both hard and soft, and with him she had felt as though she was the most special little girl in the world. Then he was gone, and her beautiful mother had figured larger in her life.

Her mother had smelled like scented soap and the contents of the glass jars and bottles on her dressing table. She had given cheerful hugs and soft kisses like the touch of butterflies' wings, and she sang the sweetest lullabies, but would never sing them long enough. Georgiana used to lie awake in her bed, smelling her mother's sweet scent long after she had left the room.

They had been poor, but Georgiana only remembered her mother speaking of it when she turned Georgiana's dresses. But then Georgiana was at Miss Silby's Academy, left to remember her mother's promises that it would be a better and happier place for her until they could be together again.

Miss Silby's had meant the loss of her mother, just as the happy time with her mother had come after her father's death. Miss Silby's had given her an education and safety, but with her mother gone it became her livelihood, its coil tightening around her, ensuring no escape.

Now that happiness beckoned again, she found her confidence and security stripped away in exchange for all the trappings of wealth and status that were not her due.

"Who am I to be?" she asked aloud of the empty room.

A knock came at her door. It startled her.

"Come in."

It was the butler, Dawes, carrying a silver salver. Upon it was a visiting card. Still somewhat shaken by Dawes's almost prophetic appearance, she picked up the card.

"He states that Lady Estcott desires him to see you."

The card said HUGH EDMUND FITZADAM, THE VIS-
COUNT RYBURN.

"I assure you that Lady Estcott approves. I am
your tutor, am I not?"

Gazing upward at his very handsome, altogether
unreadable face, Georgiana hesitated beside Lord Ryburn's glossy black phaeton. Under the brim of his
beaver hat, his tawny curls blew softly in the breeze.
His topaz eyes, like pools of golden liqueur, held her
mesmerized. She felt a glowing warmth begin inside
as though she was drunk with him.

Her heart shuddered. And then, she felt a kind of
settling, as if she might let go the bonds of her class
and speak to him as she felt she must. "Yes, you
are my tutor, sir." She paused. "But you are also a
single gentleman."

He blinked, and for the barest moment an aware-
ness flashed in his eyes. She had said something he
did not expect. "I am the Viscount Ryburn, Lady
Estcott's great-nephew. I shall also point out that this
is an open carriage and offers no threat to your
reputation."

Georgiana felt her face growing warm, and the accompanying mortification rendered her very self-
conscious. Nevertheless, she held his stare. "I am
indeed sorry if you are offended, sir. I am merely
exercising necessary discretion, as you yourself have
taught me to do."

His eyes flickered, and then his expression softened.

"You are correct to do so. I quite approve. Now, you may set aside your concerns and allow me to assist you onto the seat before my horse goes lame from standing." Then he smiled.

As quickly as that, her reservations seemed unfounded, and she let him take her hand. Holding her skirt, she made the two steps into the vehicle, heart jumping, feeling nothing but his strong, gloved hand clasping hers.

"There!" He leapt up beside her and took up the reins. "We are off, then. I thought we should tour the gardens today—they are a sight to see. There are some matters we may discuss, as well."

Georgiana then remembered Miss Hartley, and wondered what the young woman would think of Lord Ryburn taking his great-aunt's ward for a drive. She reasoned that the lady would see no cause for concern whatsoever, given their difference in status, but as she could not know, Georgiana decided to dismiss her thoughts.

"Should you like to see Kensington Park or Green Park?"

"I should like to see St. George's."

He glanced at her. "Very well. We shall go by way of Green Park. It is a pleasant spot."

"Thank you. I do appreciate the outing, sir."

"You may thank Lady Estcott, then." He hesitated.

"You are welcome, Miss Marland," he said in a kinder voice. He set the horse in motion.

Those were the last words he said for the length of Park Lane, and Georgiana had to content herself with gazing at the grand houses to her left and the vista of Hyde Park to their right. While entertained by the sights from an open carriage, she felt uneasy, and knew that Lord Ryburn was the cause.

They drove through the entrance of Green Park, and Georgiana was immediately taken by the pleasant expanse of green. It was quieter here than at Hyde Park and more peaceful. There were cows grazing, awaiting their mistresses at milking time; there were nurses with their gamboling charges; there were horses and riders taking leisurely exercise. Georgiana took a deep breath of the fresh air.

"Pleasant, is it not?" asked Lord Ryburn.

"Very much so. It is like the country, and yet it is here, in the middle of London."

A pair of children, a tiny girl in a pinafore and bonnet and a boy only slightly older, caught Georgiana's attention. The boy was examining something in the grass, a bug or some other such creature, and the girl dropped down beside him. The nurse was at the girl's side immediately, however, and caught her by the hand and drew her up.

Georgiana knew the nurse; she was Jane Southard, a girl Georgiana had taught at Miss Silby's.

"Please stop. I am acquainted with that young

woman." Georgiana looked at Lord Ryburn's face, which she could see only in profile as he continued to drive.

"Miss Marland, that young woman is a servant. Your situation now is somewhat different."

For a moment Georgiana was speechless. Then she found her voice. "Perhaps my situation is different, but that cannot alter the life I have lived or my friendships. I can see no harm in inquiring after the health of a former student."

"But I can. You may not converse with nurses in parks, no more than you may with demireps on street corners. It is not acceptable." Lord Ryburn drove on.

Georgiana sat back, feeling offended and provoked. She could see no advantage to pursuing the conversation, however, as Lord Ryburn would win. She now doubted more than ever that she would find happiness in this new life.

Time passed as they drove on in silence, save for Lord Ryburn occasionally pointing out landmarks and other items of interest. Georgiana could not even appreciate the majesty of St. George's when they passed it, so deep was her hurt. It was not until the neighborhood began to look strangely familiar that she took notice once more.

"Where are we going?"

"Can you not tell?"

"I would rather you inform me."

She feared she did know. But as he turned up the street to Miss Silby's Academy, she became certain.

"I thought that perhaps you would like a glimpse of your former home," he said. He slowed the phaeton to a walk as they approached the modest building housing Miss Silby's. The narrow street, the humble structures—all were familiar to Georgiana, but now she saw them with new eyes. It appeared poorer than before, both meaner and smaller, and her heart ached.

Lord Ryburn stopped the phaeton in front of the school, gazed at it, and then looked at Georgiana. His eyes spoke volumes.

Georgiana gripped her hands tightly in her lap. "What do you wish from me?"

"Why, nothing at all."

"I am certain there is something." She hesitated, and when he did not respond, she felt her stomach twist. "Are you attempting to frighten me?"

He blinked. For a moment he looked surprised. "Of course not. I thought you might enjoy the visit."

Georgiana drew a breath and held his golden gaze. "I think you do not like me, Lord Ryburn. I think that you resent my presence. You have made your point. I should like to go home now—if my home is indeed still with Lady Estcott."

She knew he was taken aback. There was no misunderstanding the look that flashed over his face; then he urged the horse onward.

73

"You misunderstand me," he said at last. "If I have done anything, it was to point out to you the difference between where you were and where you are now, and consequently that different behavior is required of you. You can no longer be the young woman who resided here. You must put away your life at this place, as though it never was."

"But that is not possible. I cannot forget my past."

"I do not mean for you to forget. But you must not bring it to the fore. You must never again speak of your humble beginnings, or recognize anyone in public who is connected to them. This must be understood."

Georgiana's heart throbbed in her throat, and she feared she would be sick. *Nonsense. I must not be overthrown by such talk as this. I must not allow him to intimidate me.* She must respect his station, but one's place in life was not everything.

Watching the street ahead so as to avoid his gaze, she chose her words carefully. "I am very grateful to Lady Estcott that she chose to be of use to me and aid me in finding a better place in life. But whatever I do affects my own welfare and no one else's. I shall do the best that I can. For the rest, I beg you to accept and forgive."

A long pause accentuated his displeasure. At last, he responded, "My dear Miss Marland, indeed, what you do does *not* affect you alone. Lady Estcott's reputation, and indeed my own, stand at risk. If I am opposed to you in any respect, it is on this head alone. It is imperative that you understand."

She looked at him in surprise. "I, affect the reputations of Lady Estcott and yourself? This cannot be! I am no one to have such power!"

"You have been accepted as family, and you are represented by my aunt. You are thus expected by society to hold to certain standards, and if you fail to do so, the injury will be to Lady Estcott and all of her family—including my father and me."

Georgiana drew a breath. "How very . . . odd."

He gave a soft snort, almost as if he had choked back a chuckle. "Odd!" he exclaimed. "I have just explained how the entire family's reputation turns upon the standing of one member, who in this argument is yourself, and you say it is odd! It is how society works, Miss Marland."

"In any case, I do not see how I can be such a threat. You may think little of my upbringing, but I have been taught a good deal more than you know."

"Miss Marland . . . " He turned up a tree-lined row and slowed the horse's pace. "You do not see all of the pitfalls. Indeed, I doubt that a single faux pas of yours could bring down the family. . . . It would likely need to be something of a more major sort. Perhaps I should tell you that I have been attempting to locate your mother. Your *connections* will impact upon your reputation every bit as much as anything you can do yourself—just as your reputation will now impact my family."

"My mother? But I have known nothing of her for years!"

"You told us that she is dead."

"Yes, because—"

"But that is not true, is it? You have no idea whether she is dead or alive."

Georgiana's mouth turned dry and her hands cold. She was afraid, and yet she did not know what she feared. "I—I have believed her to be dead. I can think of no other reason . . . why she—she never came back."

Tears threatened, and she blinked rapidly. She *must* not cry. Before Lord Ryburn, she must never cry!

"You see, then," he continued in a calmer voice, "that you have told an untruth, and I have had cause to question you. No harm may come of it if I can discover no ill of your mother—but if there is an unsavory secret, it will be a disaster to your reputation."

She did not respond. She could not trust her voice.

"So, Miss Marland, do you know anything of your mother?"

She wanted to answer. She wanted to tell him anything to take away his aloofness, that arrogant self-righteousness. She wanted to tell him he was wrong . . . but he was not.

"Miss Marland?"

She heard his voice, but could not look at him. She was struggling mightily to control the tears that urgently fought to come . . . that *had* come, for they were slipping down her face with no concern whatsoever for her dignity. She bowed her head and covered her eyes with one hand, and let not a sound escape.

The horse stopped. She felt Lord Ryburn lean close.

"Here. Allow me." He lifted her hand gently away from her eyes and began dabbing her face with a handkerchief.

A small sob escaped her. How dare he be kind now!

"I did not mean to be unfeeling. I have a way of wanting something, and then the devil take whosoever stands in my way. I forget myself."

She sobbed again, and cursed this weakness. She was not weak, and she would not have him think so.

"At times I am completely oblivious of the finer emotions. . . . Aunt Estcott will tell you. I did not realize I was provoking you so."

The warmth of his closeness embraced her like a wool shawl; the scent of his cologne made her senses swim. She knew not how to think of him, and certainly not how to behave; she was certain she would not even if she had undergone years of his exacting instruction. She only knew that her emotions defied reason and would not let her think.

"Come, you must speak to me. Tell me what you wish. I shall make no defense."

Georgiana swallowed. She heard the rumbling, clopping sound of a passing carriage. She smelled damp earth and horse and a whiff of the sweet scent of daffodils.

She opened her eyes.

He leaned very close, gazing into her face, and his topaz eyes were softer than she had ever seen them. She felt touched and held by them, even more than she had felt his gentle touch upon her face.

"I—I shall tell you what I know," she said.

Chapter Six

"My mother was born and raised in Hampshire. Her maiden name was Ware. I know nothing of my grandparents, save that they owned a small property there. My grandfather was a farmer, I believe, although I never heard my mother say the words. I do not think she wished for me to know."

"Do you know where she and your father were married?"

"I do not. But I believe they met in Portsmouth."

They were driving slowly along St. James's Park, where the well-dressed could be seen walking at a stately pace. Georgiana, while aware of the pretty view, was very much absorbed in the telling of her memories, and the new sensation of Lord Ryburn listening to her, intently yet sympathetically.

"Hm. My aunt seems to know nothing except the contents of a letter she received from your mother, detailing your father's death. At the time it seemed you were living in London."

Surprise made her turn to him. "My mother wrote to Lady Estcott?"

It was his turn to look surprised, and then rueful. "I am sorry—I supposed that you knew. Of course, you were very young when it occurred. Yes, she did write, apparently to convey the news."

Georgiana maintained her gaze for a moment, but his expression admitted nothing more. But Georgiana did know how they had been left, and guessed her mother's purpose in writing to her late husband's most notable relative was something more than conveying news. "She did not mention our circumstances?"

He looked away from her and gazed at the street ahead. "That I do not recall." He hesitated, and she sensed he felt ill at ease. "She may have done. I saw the letter but once."

Georgiana glanced away from him and watched the pedestrians in the Birdcage Walk along the park. Her emotions coiled within her as she realized how her mother must have felt to put a desperate appeal upon paper to a lady she did not know . . . and who ultimately did not respond.

"We had nothing," she said quietly. "I was too young to understand then, but I remember moving to a small set of rooms." *And I remember my mother weeping*.

"I am very sorry for that, Miss Marland. I truly wish your fate had been kinder."

She wondered if fate had ever been unkind to him. Somehow it seemed unlikely, but when she looked back at his profile, so calm and stoic, she knew she would not learn the answer.

"Your mother placed you at Miss Silby's Academy when, Miss Marland?"

"I was eleven years old."

"Then she had a means of support at that time, sufficient to afford the school."

Georgiana realized that, but had never been certain how it had come about. When she became old enough to understand, she had not wanted to discover the reason. "I know that, sir."

There was a long hesitation before he spoke again. Georgiana stared at the pleasantly engaged people upon the walk that they passed, wishing that she, like they, could have nothing upon her mind but sheer, glorious enjoyment.

"You last heard from her approximately three years ago, I understand."

"Yes. She sent a letter to the school saying that she could no longer pay. To me, she wrote her good-bye."

Georgiana's eyes began to fill again, and she fought it. Mercifully, Lord Ryburn said nothing for a moment, and she was able to assuage the threatening flood of tears.

"Miss Marland, I must tell you that your mother's financial situation may have forced her to circumstances you would not wish to know. Nevertheless, I must discover what the truth is. Do you understand?"

"Yes."

"I do not wish to do you harm. In actual fact, the best way to avoid it is to learn as much as I can, so as to see what might be done. Will you trust me in this?"

Georgiana drew a deep breath and made her decision. "I will not say that I trust you, Lord Ryburn; but you may do what I cannot. If she is alive, I desire that you find her. I do not care what may happen to me. What I want most is to see her again."

"I say, old fellow—I hear that old Strathmore is calling upon Miss Hartley."

Hugh finished settling himself at his table at White's and looked pointedly at his friend, Lord Winston, who sat opposite him. As usual, Winston had the nerve to smile in amusement. "A favor, if you will," Hugh said. "Do nothing more on my behalf. Ask no questions and do no listening at doors. Furthermore, be silent. I should love you for it."

"Ah, but you already do love me, Hugh, so there is no reward in that! And as a friend, I really must pay attention to your best interests. Even if it costs me—and you must hear this—even if it costs me countless minutes sitting in Lady Etherington's drawing room, in a hard chair behind a marble statue of Diana, listening to Lady Hartley and Lady Strongweld gossip."

"An unnecessary sacrifice."

"It was as boring as could be. I thought I should have to rise and attend to the necessary after half an hour, not to mention how much my nether region was aching. But at last the dear Lady Hartley came out with it, and I quite forgot my pain."

"You cannot conceive of how much I long for the end of this conversation."

"It seems you have not been attentive of late, and Lady Hartley said—although it pains me to reveal this—that she wonders if she is not developing a disgust of you. Imagine that! Disgust of the heir of a belted earl, with pots of money! It don't figure, but there it is."

"I at least can understand the emotion."

"You are a great deal better looking than Strathmore, too. Even if he does have good legs and appears to advantage on horseback."

"Strathmore has a very impressive lineage, and more estates than he can remember, as well."

"Do I sense a lack of interest, Hugh? And here I thought that Miss Hartley was to be the one."

Hugh sighed. As he gazed at Winston's comical

expression, he was hard put not to grin. "Winny, I capitulate. I surrender. I submit. Now, let us speak no more of Miss Hartley."

"Then you have gone off her? But you should tell me so!"

"I have not. I have only been busy. Although, I admit no interest in her other than my aunt's wishes and the fact that Miss Hartley is a highly unobjectionable young woman."

"Ah, then your heart is not in it. It is a sad state of affairs when a gentleman cannot marry where his heart is. But if that were the case, society would be exceedingly affronted."

"Just so."

"So there is a lady! Do tell! I had not thought you to be so enamored of your Miss Gray. Is there someone new?"

"I prefer not to discuss such intimate matters in public."

"Come now. The world knows who your mistresses are. The world knows who your *father's* mistresses are. Do not be such a stuffy old bore. It isn't like you."

"I have no mistress."

"Never."

"God's truth. Not since the autumn past. I parted from Miss Gray, and she is now very content with her new protector."

Winston stared at him, affecting a look of dismay.

"No wonder you are out of sorts, old fellow! Something must be done!"

Hugh knew that, in actual fact, Winston meant what he said. He was a true friend, and had been since their days at Eton. If Winston said something needed to be done to help his friend, he spoke from the heart.

Hugh accepted a glass of wine from the waiter and waited until the man was out of earshot. "My situation is by my design. It seemed best to focus on potential brides. It is just that another matter has intervened."

"And what may that be?"

At that moment, Hugh did as he had intended all along: He explained to Winston about his great-aunt's ward.

Winston listened intently without interruption until Hugh finished. When he was done, Winston leaned back in his chair and raised his brows. "That appears to be a fine kettle of fish," he said. "The chit seems to know how to take care of herself, I should say."

"No, there I cannot agree. She seems the very example of innocence. I have not ruled it out, however."

"She is to be your aunt's heiress."

"Yes, but that is not her doing."

"So you say."

"If she had an encroaching, flattering manner, my

aunt would not have put up with her. If I were to describe her behavior, I should say that she does what she is told and says little. It is not the manner of one seeking favor." He paused for a sip of wine. "Although I do sometimes wonder if she knows her mother is alive."

"So, then . . . you are playing nursemaid to her while examining her past? I am all astonishment! And what if you discover this vanished mother in a brothel? What then?"

"I am hoping that I do not discern the worst possible circumstance. But if she is a lady of blemished reputation and if it cannot be hidden . . ."

"I do not envy you, Hugh, and I assuredly can offer no solution. I can, however, offer a distraction. Have you perchance seen Lady Etherington's granddaughter?"

"She has not come my way. I do not recall my aunt recommending her."

"She is unimpeachable by all I have heard. You must be familiar with her father. Very old barony and a fine estate. Your aunt is too fine in her requirements, old fellow."

Hugh acknowledged that he would not object to meeting the young woman. But even as he spoke, he envisioned a lovely face and the most beautiful blue eyes he had ever beheld, and felt a pang of regret.

Miss Marland was a fine kettle of fish, indeed.

*   *   *

Lady Estcott was no better.

Three days had passed since Georgiana's drive with Lord Ryburn, and Lady Estcott still kept to her room. Miss Frey said that she complained of a headache, as well as an ache in her side and an irritation of the throat, and had banned Miss Frey from the room in a pet. Agnes, her maid, attended her; she refused to see the doctor.

Georgiana still had Lady Estcott's refusal to help her mother fresh in her mind, but the old lady's illness worried her. She therefore made up her mind to see what might be the matter in spite of Lady Estcott's insistence on seeing no one.

Georgiana tapped only lightly on the door to Lady Estcott's chambers, and then stepped into the room. Lady Estcott lay not on her chaise but in bed, propped up with pillows, a damp cloth across her forehead. Her eyes were closed.

"Lady Estcott, I came to see how you are feeling."

Her eyes popped open. The furrow between them remained. "Miss Marland? Did no one tell you that I will not have visitors? Go away!"

Georgiana closed the door behind her and advanced to the bedside. "I am not a visitor. I live here, and I am family."

"Miss Frey is family, and I sent *her* off." The old woman's voice was milder now, as if she was willing to be convinced.

87

"You spend many hours with Miss Frey, and one becomes out of sorts when one is ill, particularly with those one knows best." Georgiana sat in the chair near the bedside, most likely vacated by the evicted Miss Frey. "You do not know me so very well."

Lady Estcott closed her eyes once more. "So now you will speak out of turn, and take terrible advantage of a sick old woman. Be warned, I am very awake on such matters."

"No, I shall be very kind. One needs others when one is ill."

"Well, you need *me*, I suppose. You should not like to see me depart the world at such an inconvenient time, should you? Your come-out plans are not yet finished."

"I do not need a come-out."

Lady Estcott's eyes popped open again. "What? Not need a come-out? You are absurd, girl! Of course you must have one. Do you not like your new gowns? Do you not want to dance with young gentlemen and find one fit to marry? This is what one does in society!"

"I am a naval officer's daughter, and I have nothing in the world save what you give me. I am used to much less, and I did not expect to marry."

"Your situation has changed. It is more than time that you get used to what you have now! A comeout is a necessity for a young woman in your circumstances."

Georgiana gazed at the old woman's pale, lined

face and her sharp, yet hopeful eyes and felt something she had not expected to feel. Compassion.

She reached over and laid her hand over Lady Estcott's. "What is it that is bothering you? For I do not think it is only the headache."

Lady Estcott looked surprised and blinked. "I have aches and pains. I am old. What sort of question is that?"

"I think it came on rather suddenly, and I have not known you to have a headache since I have been here."

"You have scarcely been here a month."

"Miss Frey says that you have a headache only when something has upset you."

"Oh, she told you that, did she? The old gossip! Why I have her here I shall never know!"

"Of course you know. She is devoted to you. And she also said you have an irritation of the throat."

"Oh, that! I told her that so she would stop plaguing me to speak to her. I only want to be left alone!"

"There is also a pain in your side."

"That is true enough, and you are beginning to make it worse."

"I think I shall get the doctor."

"You shall do no such thing!" Lady Estcott rose up on one elbow and glared at Georgiana. "I always have a pain in my side. It is because I am old. I shall *not* see a doctor because I am old!" She fell back upon the pillows, scowling.

"Very well. Please tell me what the matter is." Georgiana curled her fingers more snugly around Lady Estcott's cold hand.

It surprised Georgiana how easy it was to cross that invisible barrier of class that she had so feared. Lady Estcott, a very high and grand lady indeed, now seemed very much like a sick child in need of comfort—and Georgiana had cared for many sick girls at Miss Silby's.

Lady Estcott sighed. Then she blinked, and Georgiana was concerned to see the shimmer of tears in her eyes.

"I have not been able to secure you vouchers to Almack's," she said.

Georgiana gazed at her, waiting for more, but nothing came. "It is only that?" she asked.

"*Only* that?" snapped Lady Estcott. Her pale face flushed, and she rose up on her elbow once more. "It means everything! You simply *must* be admitted to Almack's. It shall not make a feather's worth of difference if you are a thousand times more beautiful than Arietta's granddaughter, if you cannot get in to Almack's!"

"Lady Estcott, calm yourself." Georgiana stood and eased Lady Estcott back upon the pillows; the old lady continued to scowl at her all the while. "Who is Arietta, and why is her granddaughter so important?"

"She is not important. Not as important as Arietta believes."

"Unless I do not get vouchers to Almack's?"

Lady Estcott sighed, and as it escaped her she relaxed at last. "Yes."

Georgiana sat down once more. "Tell me about Arietta, Lady Estcott. I would like to hear about her."

Lady Estcott was silent a moment. Then she drew a breath. "Sixty years ago this season, a young woman had her come-out. Seventeen forty-eight . . . that was the year. She was a *beautiful* girl. She wore a lovely, yellow silk damask gown and the sweetest matching shoes with tall, elegant heels. . . . She wore jewels in her hair, and her shoulders were as white as alabaster."

"She sounds lovely."

"She was. And the night of her come-out ball she met the most agreeable gentleman. . . . I wish you could see him the way I do. He was so handsome. So dashing. He had the most elegant legs."

Georgiana felt heat rise to her face at this shocking description, but kept her tongue. The elderly had different ways.

"He was Lord Etherington. And the young woman fell in love with him."

"And they married."

"No, they did not!" Lady Estcott's eyes flew wide open, and she glared at her.

Georgiana started. "I am sorry. I should not have interrupted—"

"Arietta married him . . . after she *stole* him from *me!*"

"Oh . . . I see."

"The vixen! She knew very well that he was court-ing me, and was well on the way to asking for my hand. Everyone expected it to happen. And then one evening she lost her heel in the garden . . . I am sure by design. And before anyone knew, they were embracing behind the dovecote!"

"You must have been very distraught."

"I could never forgive her. Never. It only mattered to her that she got him, of course. She felt no shame. She was embraced as Lady Etherington, too, once she was wed, while I—*I* was the one who suffered!"

"Was—was she very beautiful?"

"Her?" Lady Estcott's voice was contemptuous. "Some may have thought so, but *I* did not. Fair haired, no bigger than a minute . . . a washed-out little thing." She paused. "And so I married Lord Estcott in the end. But I do believe Lord Etherington always had a fondness for me."

"Oh, dear. All this time has passed, and he still breaks your heart?"

Lady Estcott gave her a sharp look. "What do you know of love, young lady? It does not wither away and die so easily. Are you thinking my marriage should have put an end to it? That is not how it is. I cared for Lord Estcott, but he never had my heart as Lord Etherington did."

Georgiana remained silent.

"I never told Estcott about Lord Etherington, of

course. I have discussed it with no one these sixty years . . . save you."

"I—I am happy that you did tell me, Lady Estcott. I assure you it will remain a secret."

"Of course it will, or I should not have told you," Lady Estcott snapped. Then her voice softened. "I never told Lord Etherington, either." She paused. "I let him wonder!"

Georgiana fought to restrain a smile, all the while feeling deep sympathy for Lady Estcott. How sad that this one thing had so embittered her. "Perhaps he knows," she offered gently.

"I should think not. He has been dead for thirty years!"

Shortly after Georgiana visited Lady Estcott in her room, Lady Estcott arose and came forth with a spring in her step and new fire in her eye. Immediately she initiated a flurry of activity, busying the servants with a top to bottom cleaning of the house, sending for merchants, consulting with her cook, and revising her invitation list for Georgiana's come-out.

The very next morning, Lady Estcott appeared dressed in the latest town fashion, looking very smart, indeed, and demanded her carriage. She refused accompaniment, so Miss Frey and Georgiana could only look on and wonder as she left. Georgiana spent the morning practicing her needlework with Miss Frey as she had been instructed to do, and by the time this was finished, she had learned a lot about the quiet companion.

Miss Frey was the daughter of a country gentleman, had nursed both her parents, and had come to Lady Estcott's several years ago after Lord Estcott had passed away. She stated that she was content, and that she and Lady Estcott went along very well. Then, Miss Frey produced a book with a little gleam in her eyes. It was a novel of the type disapproved by Lady Estcott. Miss Frey suggested that Georgiana read aloud as Miss Frey continued her needlework; and thus they were pleasantly occupied until they heard Lady Estcott's carriage return.

Lady Estcott swept into the room with astounding energy. Stripping off her black gloves, she drew a sheaf of papers from her reticule and held them in the air.

"I have them," she announced triumphantly. "I was so foolish to think Lady Jersey my friend. *She* would have denied me, or at the very least made me wait on pins and needles. But Lady Sefton has done the thing, and here we are! I should have gone to her immediately!"

"What are they?" Georgiana asked.

"The vouchers, dear," said Miss Frey.

"What could I possibly be speaking of?" cried Lady Estcott. "The vouchers to Almack's, of course!"

Chapter Seven

*G*eorgiana dreamed that she was dressed in a golden gown as soft as gossamer, descending a golden stair resting on rose-colored clouds. Below her waited an endless throng of ladies and gentlemen; the room seemed to have no walls and go on forever. Above her was a moonlit sky and nothing more. She floated down the stairs, and the moon grew brighter. As she neared the bottom, it became light as day.

Suddenly, a woman reached out from the crowd and pointed accusingly at her. "I know who she is! She is no lady—she is a teacher at Miss Silby's Academy!"

A hush fell over the crowd. Then a little girl asked, "Where is your mother?"

Georgiana looked around herself, wondering where her mother had gone. Her mother had been with her in Hyde Park earlier in the day; then, she remembered. Her mother had entered a closed carriage with a strange gentleman and gone away with him, leaving her alone.

Lord Ryburn stepped out from the crowd of guests. He stared at her with a look of condemnation on his face. "I know where her mother is . . . and I know *who* she is."

Everyone stared at her—hundreds of faces, shocked and outraged—waiting for Lord Ryburn to tell the terrible secret.

Then she awoke.

Georgiana lay in bed, filled with a horrible foreboding. When she told Lord Ryburn she wanted him to find her mother, she had meant it. Though she wished with all her heart to see her mother again, she believed that all he might find was the truth about her fate—and possibly with it a dark secret.

It was this that she feared: the idea of confronting the finality of her mother's death and with it an awful truth—without the comfort of seeing her mother's face again and without feeling her mother's arms surrounding her with love. Instead, she would have only anguished questions for which she would never have answers.

With this double grief, she would have to face Lady Estcott's society and smile, pretending she was something other than what she was. Society would never understand if they were to learn that her mother had sacrificed her honor to live, and in their eyes she herself would become something much worse than a former teacher from Miss Silby's Academy.

Lady Estcott would be ruined, as well.

Georgiana stared into the darkness until dawn, trying to think of a way to convince Lady Estcott to give up her grand plans for her, but now that her debut was to be at Almack's, Lady Estcott seemed more determined than ever. Georgiana could, of course, tell Lady Estcott her fear, but another fear loomed larger. She was afraid of her mother's possible fate—and that it could await her should Lady Estcott put her out without a reference. There would be no returning to Miss Silby's if her reputation was ruined.

How she wished Lord Ryburn had never spoken to her, had not made her see that Lady Estcott's generosity came with such peril. And . . . how she wished he had never shown her how gentle he could be, and how compassionate, when an impassible chasm lay between them.

She did not know if she could rival the beautiful granddaughter of Lady Etherington, but she did know that like Lady Estcott, she would lose the battle for love.

In the following days, Lady Escott was in such a whirl of activity that there was no doubt whatsoever that she had recovered. Her recovery, as Georgiana knew, was very much due to the precious vouchers she had obtained from Lady Sefton, securing Georgiana's admission to Almack's. It was one more thing to force her more prominently into the eye of the *haut ton*, and one even more frightening than Lady Estcott's plans for a private celebration . . . especially now when her evening at Almack's was upon her.

Now, as she gazed into her looking glass, she saw the imposter staring back at her. Agnes, behind her, drew mightily on the corset laces. Georgiana seized the edge of her dressing table for support.

"Must it be so tight?"

"Yes, miss. Her ladyship said to be sure it is tightened properly. Tonight is very important, she said."

"I never wore a corset laced so closely before."

"You will become used to it in time."

Agnes secured the laces and then quickly returned with the gown Georgiana was to wear that evening. First was the pale rose silk underdress, then the muslin overdress, embroidered all over with gold thread. It had short, slashed sleeves and a deep square bodice. Indeed, Georgiana had never before displayed so much bosom in public view.

"It is so very fashionable, miss," said Agnes. "Her ladyship is simply delighted with this gown. And now, you must put on her ladyship's diamond eardrops." Agnes picked up the small velvet box she had placed on the dressing table moments before, and opened it to present two small, brilliant earrings.

Georgiana's fingers trembled as she picked up each dazzling diamond and slipped them into her ears. Then Agnes handed her a pair of long, soft, kid gloves, and as Georgiana slipped them on, she turned to view her reflection once more.

A beautiful, dark-haired woman gazed back at her. Georgiana stared and blinked, as did the woman in the glass.

"This cannot be me."

"Oh, but it is!" came Lady Estcott's voice. The grande dame, dressed in deep plum satin, sailed into the room, came up to her and stopped. Then she gently clasped Georgiana's face and gazed at her.

"You are so beautiful. Oh, how I prayed for this! No one else can hold a candle to you!"

Georgiana was surprised to see tears shimmering in Lady Estcott's eyes. "I do not deserve to be dressed so," she said helplessly.

"Nonsense. I shall hear no more of that. From this moment forward, you are to think and act and speak as though you deserve it fully, for you do! There is something I want to tell you, my dear, and to-night you must know." Lady Estcott paused and gazed fondly into Georgiana's eyes. "I have made you my heiress, my dear. You will be a very rich woman. Now, get your shawl, for Lord Ryburn will be here presently. You will make me very proud tonight!"

Lord Ryburn did not like Almack's.

Lord Ryburn did not like the rules or the refreshments; he disliked wearing knee breeches; he did not like presenting himself to the exclusive multitude as a single gentleman of excellent status in need of a wife, for that was surely how he was viewed. He knew that none of the young ladies present had a chance at gaining his genuine affection, should they hope for it, for he was incapable of giving it. Life had taught him that women were fleeting things in a man's life, whether they sadly passed away or abandoned their husbands emotionally, as had happened with many of his friends.

As much as he and his father thought differently, he had to admit he was of his father's mind in one respect. Since his mother's death, his father never again sought a wife; he enjoyed women, but never attempted another lasting attachment.

Like his father, Hugh found it comfortable to enjoy a mistress for whatever length of time the liaison seemed mutually beneficial, then move on, maintaining his independence until another pleasing courtesan caught his eye. It was only the pressure to marry and produce an heir, mostly from his great-aunt, that had arrested his usual manner of pursuing life.

He had concluded that he best get the matter done with so that he could eventually return to his preferred way of being—his wife could have her freedom after the heir was born, and he would find a new mistress. Only now, Miss Hartley seemed likely to slip through his fingers while he attended to the problem of Miss Marland and fretted about the situation.

He was sorry, for he had felt that Miss Hartley, beyond being eligible, would fit with his view of married life; but he would find another if he must. He would begin a new pursuit after Miss Marland had been safely dealt with. But—most unfortunately— attending to Miss Marland meant escorting Aunt Estcott and her to Almack's tonight.

In a mood that was too far from pleasant for him to be happy with the night's prospects, he arrived at his aunt's town house and mounted the steps, feeling much like a man mounting the gallows to meet his own demise. He would give anything even now to stop his aunt from tonight's presentation of Miss Marland, as the knowledge that Miss Marland's mother was alive and in London had confirmed his deepest worry. It now seemed far too easy for Mrs. Marland to be discovered by another, and it would be only a matter of learning how far she had fallen to judge the depth of his family's scandal. But he knew, absolutely, that there would be no stopping his great-aunt now.

He was admitted into the entrance hallway by Dawes, who indicated that he was to wait while Dawes summoned the ladies. Rather than sit in the small library he endured the wait in the hall, wandering its length and back and examining the several paintings gracing its walls. At last he heard a step upon the stairs. He looked up and saw a goddess descending.

Hugh stood and stared as the vision in white gracefully made her way down the steps, one hand on the banister, the other holding the gold embroidered gown to keep from treading on it. Her raven hair was piled high on the back of her head in an intricate arrangement of loops and twists, with a thin golden ribbon woven through it in the style of a woman of ancient Rome. The sparks of fire at her ears told him she wore diamond eardrops, but there was no ornament upon her white breast.

She needs a diamond necklace. No, she does not precisely need one, but I would have her wear a diamond necklace.

She had not seen him yet. She was engaged in watching her feet, and although the effect denied sophistication, it was charming. She neared the bottom, and he swallowed. He felt very nearly tongue-tied. What in the world was the matter with him? And why was he thinking of dressing her in *diamonds*?

She looked up, and their gazes met. Her beautiful

violet blue eyes grew wide, and their light pierced him straight through. Hugh felt his heart turn over.

He moistened his lips. "Miss Marland . . . you look exquisite."

Her cheeks gained a tinge of pink, and she smiled. "Thank you. It is a surprise, is it not? I scarcely know myself."

He cleared his throat. "Ah, but one must not say so," he said gently.

"I know. But it is *you*, Lord Ryburn. I should not be quite so frank with anyone else."

He could not help but smile. The impact of her beauty upon him seemed to have punctured his careful reserve. "Very well. But have a care. Aunt Estcott will tell you that you must seem to expect admiration."

"I have already told her." Lady Estcott moved into view on the landing and began descending the lower flight of stairs. "She is stunning, is she not, Hugh? I am nearly beside myself. She is to be the belle of the season."

Hugh could not remember the last time he had seen his aunt smile—or wear any color save black. She appeared years younger and even her step was lighter.

"There is no doubt whatsoever that she will be the most beautiful woman in attendance tonight," he said.

"Not only will she be the most beautiful, she will be the most desired. Every gentleman will wish to dance with her." Lady Estcott reached the bottom of the stairs, and Hugh noticed that she was going out tonight without the aid of her silver-headed walking stick.

"Let us be going. The very last thing we want is to be late, on tonight of all nights!"

Georgiana had descended the stairs, feeling such excitement and fear she scarcely knew if her knees would support her down to the bottom step. She was to see Lord Ryburn, and with all her foolish heart hoped he would be delighted with her tonight. When at last she looked up, she saw him there awaiting her, wearing a black coat and breeches, his snowy white cravat sporting the glint of a single diamond, and his eyes holding the glow of a thousand.

He admired her—and then, he told her she looked exquisite. Her heart sailed upward, and she felt such a surge of happiness that she cared not what else he said. It was worth it all for just this one moment.

He handed her into the coach and she sat by Lady Estcott, finding the lady's troubling revelation of moments ago surprisingly easy to bear. Tonight, she would live a dream, the like of which she might not have again. It would not be spoiled by useless worries about tomorrow.

The carriage arrived at last at Almack's. The moment she stepped into the grand ballroom would be forever emblazoned on her mind. It was enormous, with gilt columns and mirrors, classically styled paneling and ornate plasterwork, and lit by beautiful crystal chandeliers suspended from the ceiling.

At the entrance to the grand ballroom, she saw that they were about to encounter some illustrious persons, and quickly made certain that her mouth was closed.

Their party paused. Lady Estcott exchanged greetings with the lady who met them. ". . . And this is Miss Marland. Miss Marland, Lady Sefton."

Georgiana curtsied.

"You look very lovely," the lady said.

"Thank you."

And then they were in the ballroom. Georgiana realized that her heart was beating so hard and rapidly that her chest must have been visibly bobbing.

She had done it. She had almost expected to be barred at the door, but she was here, in Almack's on a Wednesday night, surrounded by the elite of society. It hardly seemed possible.

She looked around for Lord Ryburn, but he had left to secure them chairs. Lady Estcott, still breathing rather rapidly after the long flights of stairs, now held Georgiana's arm.

"I shall tell you with whom you are allowed to

dance," she said presently. "Lady Sefton has matched you with appropriate partners, and there must be no error."

"I understand."

"I am fairly well pleased with the gentlemen, all in all," she continued. "At another time you shall have more choice in the matter."

"I am happy to be here. I am very far from any further desire, I can assure you."

"That is good. Now, I see Hugh returning, and I must have a chair. Come along."

Lord Ryburn had found seats for them near the musician's balcony. Lady Estcott sat with relief and Georgiana with pent-up expectation. She did not have long to wait. A young man with red hair presented himself to Lady Estcott, who introduced him to Georgiana as Lord Talbot, one of the gentlemen with whom she would dance.

She entered the set of the country-dance with some nervousness, but she knew she was equal to it. When the dance started, she quickly found herself taken up in the pleasure of the movements and the music, without noticing much else at first. As she moved up the dance, however, she finally placed the petite, blond young woman with a delicate face and a beautiful smile. She was Miss Etherington, the granddaughter of Lady Estcott's old rival.

Georgiana watched her covertly after that. The girl seemed playful and sweet, and she was light on her feet, graceful as a butterfly going from flower to flower. Georgiana experienced the unfamiliar sensation of gentlemen's stares, but it soon became clear that Miss Etherington shared this, as well.

After the first dance Lord Talbot guided her back to Lady Estcott, thanked her kindly, and bowed himself away. It was then that Georgiana noticed that Lady Estcott was as white as death.

"Lady Estcott! Are you quite well? Is there anything that you need?" Georgiana sank down in the chair beside Lady Estcott and took one of her hands.

"No, I need nothing."

Georgiana noticed that a barely touched glass of lemonade rested on the table before them.

"Should we not go?"

Abruptly Lady Estcott inhaled a deep breath and turned a severe look upon her. "Absolutely not! I shall not let *that woman* ruin your come-out! It is not to be thought of!"

"That woman—?" But Georgiana already suspected that she knew which woman Lady Estcott meant.

"Lady Etherington. That—that sly thing is presenting her granddaughter tonight, of all nights, and I must suffer to breathe the same air! I never expected such bad luck!"

Georgiana gazed about the room of patrons, at last spying a petite lady, dressed in black satin and net, seated a distance away, in conversation with a gentleman. It was indeed the lady from the carriage in Hyde Park. Georgiana was little surprised, seeing as her granddaughter was present.

"At least she is seated some distance away. I am surprised you perceived her."

"My dear, I always attend these affairs with a lorgnette. It is of no use whatsoever to be here if I cannot see!"

"I am sorry. I did not know. I have not seen you use it before. I supposed you did not need one."

"I try not to, but this room is much too large to avoid it. Not that I have difficulty in knowing *her* face. I knew her in an instant in Hyde Park."

"The carriage was quite close to ours."

"Do not contradict me, young lady! I knew *her*. It was her granddaughter I could not see!"

Georgiana fell silent, concluding there was little she could do, and waited with as much equanimity as she could muster for her next dance. It was not long in coming . . . but it was entirely spoiled by Lord Ryburn standing up in the same dance with Miss Etherington.

The dance began, and she forced herself through the movements, smiling as well as she could. When the pattern of the dance brought her face-to-face with Lord Ryburn, she smiled some more, but felt the insincerity of it. She told herself that he was dancing with Miss Etherington out of duty, for in all probability he was; but the young woman's beauty and style were compelling, and she could not expect him to be immune. Then, in addition to that, Miss Etherington was the daughter of a peer. Georgiana must not forget she was a naval officer's daughter and a former teacher, and all of Lady Estcott's machinations could not make her into what she was not. Not even declaring her an heiress could change that.

And . . . after tonight, Georgiana strongly suspected that her rags-to-riches odyssey would not last, and none of her yearnings or fears would matter. Fate would surely hurl devastation into her path once more.

The dance ended at long last, and Mr. Underwood, her partner, began to walk her back to Lady Estcott. To Georgiana's surprise, Lady Estcott was not in her chair.

Georgiana looked about rapidly, then ruefully back at Mr. Underwood. "I do not see Lady Estcott."

"Nor do I," he said lightly. "Never fear—I shall find her. You may be certain that she has not gone very far."

Mr. Underwood was a gentle, middle-aged gentleman with a good fortune and an old name, the latter of which she had learned from Lady Estcott; but only his gentlemanly care of her mattered to her now. It would not do for her to be wandering about in the ballroom alone.

"She was not feeling quite well earlier."

"Ah, but I do believe I have spied her."

There she was, indeed, standing up in conversation with Lady Etherington.

"Oh, dear," she said softly.

"I beg your pardon, I did not hear what you said."

"Oh, it was nothing at all." She smiled disarmingly at him.

It certainly was something. Even before they drew close, Georgiana could tell that all was not well. Both ladies were stone-faced, furious beneath a veneer of civility. Georgiana could only wonder and worry about the content of their conversation until they came within earshot.

". . . do not know that . . . ever heard . . . Marland spoken of."

Georgiana surged ahead, nearly towing the surprised Mr. Underwood behind her.

". . . was a hero in His Majesty's Navy. He was to be decorated . . . tragically killed before it could happen."

"What of her mother's family?"

Georgiana arrived at Lady Estcott's side. "I am returned, Lady Estcott," she said somewhat breathlessly. "It was a lovely dance."

Relief flashed into Lady Estcott's eyes. "And so it was. You dance very well, my dear."

From the corner of her eye, Georgiana spotted the blond head of Lord Ryburn above the crowd, returning Miss Etherington to her grandmother. Her heart leapt in panic.

"Do let us go immediately to sit down. I must rest for a moment and have a drink of lemonade."

Not a moment too soon, Lady Estcott turned away to accompany her—without seeing her nephew and Miss Etherington. Georgiana kept Lady Estcott's attention with small talk until they were at a safe distance, and privately thanked the angel who had seen fit to allay further upset to her lady sponsor that evening.

She thanked the angel for herself, as well, for at this moment she did not feel at all capable of facing Lord Ryburn.

Chapter Eight

"You escorted your aunt and Miss Marland this evening," said Lady Etherington, smiling.

Hugh gazed down at the small lady and sensed that her size belied her power. Her granddaughter's silvery blue eyes sparkled, but on her grandmother, they glinted like polished steel. "That is correct. Miss Marland is also making her come-out tonight, as is your lovely granddaughter."

Lady Etherington's smile grew, and she clearly looked delighted. "She is lovely. I told my son that she is the best thing he has done. You do know Lord Etherington, my son, do you not? I am sure you have met him. He does not frequent London often. I have urged him to become active in the House of Lords, but he is more interested in crops and horses and making his land turn a profit. But he did marry a very beautiful wife, and he is very nearly as handsome as his father—and so Miss Etherington's beauty is no surprise."

Hugh nodded. He then turned to Miss Etherington. "Your mother did not come to town?"

"Oh, no—in fact, she is—not well enough to travel at present."

"I am sorry."

"Oh, no, do not be sorry," said Lady Etherington. "My daughter-in-law is in the family way! We expect an addition to the family by summer's end. Her mother is extremely healthy, as is Miss Etherington. It is very fortunate."

"Yes, of course."

He looked down again at the pretty face of Miss Etherington. He liked the laughing light in her eyes. Perhaps the search for Miss Hartley's replacement would not be so very difficult, after all.

He felt another stab of regret. *Miss Marland.* But it did not matter what his feelings were; he must choose above her, even if her reputation did not shatter like a house of cards.

"Is Mrs. Marland in town?"

Hugh's attention was quickly brought back to the older lady. "I—I do not know." *Think, man, think!* "Miss Marland has not been with her mother for some years. Lady Estcott thought it best to take her turn and sponsor her this season."

"I see. Hm. Well, some mothers may lack that certain instinct, I suppose. I, for one, would never have allowed a child of mine to be brought up beneath another's wing. But I am certain Mrs. Marland had her reasons. We should not be too quick to judge, should we?"

Hugh parted from the ladies Etherington at last, feeling somewhat uncomfortable and suspecting that there had been something in their communication that he had not quite understood. Then it was time for the next dance, and he dismissed his misgivings.

Georgiana stood up for another dance, then for another and another. She quite liked a gentleman or two, but she always felt a stab of fear when she considered her future. Regardless of Lady Estcott's plans, she could not count on carefree days of bliss ahead. While the question of her mother lingered, she was not safe here.

Where had her determination to enjoy the evening gone? She had started the night with such hopes. Perhaps she had only just recovered her senses after the double shock of Lady Estcott's announcement that she would be her heiress, and Lord Ryburn's golden eyes glowing in approval and admiration.

She felt that she would never see his eyes so warm again.

She returned from yet another dance, expecting to see Lady Estcott still sitting tall, the iron rod of nobility in her spine, the cool haughtiness still in her eyes. But this time, Lady Estcott was not alone. An elderly gentleman, tall and thin with a regal bearing and a sturdy gold-headed cane, sat with her.

Lady Estcott spied her. "My dear," said Lady Estcott, smiling. "This gentleman is Lord Felstone. We were once very good friends. Lord Felstone, my ward and cousin, Miss Marland."

He stood, a slow process as, leaning heavily on the cane, he straightened to his full height. "How do you do, Miss Marland," he said gravely. "I am happy to have the acquaintance of any connection of Lady Estcott. And if I dare contradict the lady, we are *still* good friends, even though we have not seen each other in years."

"Sit down, dear. Lord Felstone, are you trying to make me blush? It cannot be done. I am too old and too determined to maintain my dignity."

The old gentleman pulled out a chair for Georgiana, and once she was seated, he turned a slight smile on Lady Estcott.

"Anything you say, my dear lady, I shall accept with no protest whatsoever. But I still may think that you are the loveliest lady ever born, and still with a sweet maiden's heart."

"Now, you positively must stop. You must not shock Miss Marland."

Georgiana could tell, however, that Lady Estcott was excessively pleased, and it was not only because color had returned to the old lady's face.

"How are you acquainted?" she asked.

"Ah. Shall I explain?" said Lord Felstone. "We were friends of the same gentleman once, a very long time ago. He had a prior claim, and I foolishly allowed her to escape." A light in his eyes told Georgiana that he said it all in good humor.

"It does not matter," Lady Estcott said rather sharply. Then she added, "Eventually I married, and Lord Felstone married, and that put an end to our acquaintance."

"But there is no reason not to resume it now, I should think," Lord Felstone said.

"I do not go to parties as I used to do. It is for Miss Marland that I am here tonight."

"I do not go about so very much myself anymore. Perhaps you would like to take a drive with me very soon."

"I do not—that is, I—"

"I shall call on you."

"That would be lovely."

They exchanged parting words, and at last Lord Felstone rose and walked away slowly, with a decided limp and a back as straight as a ramrod.

Georgiana looked at Lady Estcott, who was gazing after him. "I like him very much," Georgiana said.

"What?"

"Lord Felstone. I like him very much."

"He is too old for you, dear."

"Yes, I know." She smiled. "But I do believe he is fond of you."

Lady Estcott snapped her gaze to Georgiana's face, looking fierce. "That is not a matter for you to speak of. In any case, you are quite wrong. Lord Felstone is a very fine gentleman—one who knows how to treat a lady with respect—and that is all. Men of my time know chivalry!"

Georgiana fell silent, but privately she was very much of another opinion about Lady Estcott and Lord Felstone.

What if I were responsible for destroying her happiness yet again?

Georgiana's heart grew heavier than it had ever been, and she was ready for her lovely evening to be over.

Lady Estcott returned to Park Lane with a smile on her face. Georgiana, while glad to see that smile, retired to her room with her mind abuzz with worry. The worries accompanied her to bed, and she sorted through them all as she stared up at the starless night of the canopy.

People had asked about her mother. A simple reply that she was deceased would not suffice forever. Lady Estcott, clever as she was, would fashion some response, but it was not inconceivable that someone would not be satisfied. She wondered how Lady Estcott expected a potential husband to be content with a half answer.

As for her father . . . she wondered at what she

had heard Lady Estcott tell Lady Etherington. A hero in His Majesty's Navy? About to be decorated? Georgiana had never heard those things, and she wondered if this was something she had never known, or something Lady Estcott had designed. She would have to learn the answer on the morrow.

In spite of her worries, her sad yearning for Lord Ryburn, the thing she had most sought to avoid, permeated all of her thoughts. He had seemed to change from a stern taskmaster to a much warmer gentleman, with a smile in his eyes for her, a gentle squeeze of her hand when they crossed in the dance. He had not been partnered with her this evening, but he had acknowledged her, telling her that she had not been mistaken about the way he looked at her when she had first encountered him that evening at the bottom of Lady Estcott's stairs.

Yet he had smiles for Miss Etherington, too.

Georgiana slept very late and awoke with the high sun of late morning peeking through the window draperies. She sat up and drew back the bed curtain. The room was cool and a fire had been lit in the grate. She caught the scent of something sweet, and realized it was the scent of flowers.

This was enough to energize her. She climbed out of bed and found her robe and slippers on the chair waiting for her. Then she started to walk around the bed and saw the source of the scent.

On her dressing table, her writing desk, and on

the occasional table near the fireplace were vases upon vases of flowers—perhaps a dozen in all. But the one that most caught her eye was the enormous bouquet of roses, jonquils, and lavender on her dressing table. She padded over to it and picked up the card.

To the loveliest flower of the evening. My best wishes, L.R.

Lord Ryburn had sent her flowers.

She sat in her dressing table chair and nearly dissolved into tears, but she could hardly tell whether they were of grief or happiness. Then she rang her bell.

Her new maid, Susan, answered her call and entered the room, bearing yet another beautiful bouquet. "Is it not lovely?" she said happily. Georgiana could see that the young woman was nearly bursting with excitement and doing her best to contain it.

"Good morning, Susan. Who are those from?"

Susan brought the flowers, a mix of lilac sprays and white lilies, to her. Georgiana opened the card.

Best wishes to a lovely young lady. Yours, L. Felstone

"How kind," Georgiana murmured. She wondered what flowers he had sent to Lady Estcott.

She looked up at Susan, and saw that the poor girl was longing to know more about the evening at Almack's but had been taught not to ask. Susan, who had not been trusted with dressing her for the great evening, had not even seen Georgiana's gown. "It was a lovely evening, Susan," Georgiana said. "The most beautiful night of my life."

"Oh, miss, I thought it must be! Agnes said you were so beautiful!"

Georgiana did not utter a reprimand for the personal comment though she knew that she should. "Please bring me a plain morning gown. I do not care which one."

"Oh, the yellow figured one!"

"It will do."

Georgiana arrived downstairs to find Lady Estcott already in the breakfast room, although it was early after so late an evening. She had an unusual rosiness in her cheeks and a sparkle in her eyes, and she was perusing the morning *Times*.

"Good morning, Lady Estcott."

"Good morning, my dear! What a fine day it is. It seems last evening has already been remarked upon, and you have been mentioned! Just listen: 'Miss Marland wore white muslin, embroidered all over in gold, over rose silk, and altogether was the prettiest young woman to make her entrée this evening as her beauty was much remarked upon.' "

"My goodness!" Georgiana paused in the act of

pouring her tea at the buffet and looked at Lady Estcott. "How can this be? I am certain there were others there a great deal more beautiful."

"I disagree. And in any event, it only matters what is said." She laid the paper aside. "You must have noticed the flowers. I made sure to see them before they were delivered to your room, and all who ought to have sent them did so."

"Ought to have?" Georgiana came to the table and sat opposite Lady Estcott.

"Every gentleman you danced with, every gentleman who ought to show you interest. A few which were only congratulatory, to be sure, but the others are of significance."

Georgiana supposed that Lord Ryburn's flowers were only congratulatory, and suppressed the new surge of sadness at this.

"You will have callers, so you must be dressed for the occasion. We will be at home today. I would like to see you in the pale blue muslin with the netting. Agnes will do your hair."

Georgiana saw that there would be no rest for her, and although she had expected it might be so, her heart fell. How could she look ahead to this with anything but anxiety now, when it surely must end?

"I have also been thinking of the ball I had been planning to give for you. Now that you have come out at Almack's, I believe I might make some alterations. I have been thinking it would be a good thing to have the affair at my nephew's home—Lord Wyndgrave's residence, that is. And I think it may be made a more pleasing affair if it is a musical evening, as well, and you may play the pianoforte."

"But I do not play for an audience, Lady Estcott."

"My dear—now, you shall."

Lord Felstone drove his rig slowly down the street, ignoring the drivers who passed him. He was fully capable of driving to an inch, but at his advanced age it was much wiser to cross the bumps and holes slowly to afford as much comfort as possible to his old bones.

Lord Felstone thought as he drove. He found driving very good for thinking; the activity seemed to stimulate his aged brain. He no longer made the claim that he was as sharp as he ever was, but he did know others who had become a good deal *less* sharp than he, so he generally took as much opportunity as possible to keep his head in good working order. However, today he had another purpose. He was thinking about Miss Adderly.

No, not Miss Adderly, he told himself. Lady Estcott. He did not blame himself for that error, however, for all of his memories of her were from the days when she *was* Miss Adderly. She was young and sprightly and full of fun then; he had never seen light dance as it did in her eyes. In his mind he saw her as he had that first evening he met her, when his young heart had reached out and lost itself to her.

That was before his best friend, Lord Etherington, had looked her way, so in under a half hour he had given her up. He was a second son and a rising army officer, and Lord Etherington was an earl, having already inherited his father's title. Etherington was deuced handsome, too, and even a fair-looking fellow like he, Felstone, had been, was no competition, had he but a title, as well.

Miss Adderly became Lady Estcott when he was away on campaign, and he returned home astounded that Etherington had married Miss Sewell instead, for he had thought Etherington all but engaged to Miss Adderly. In any event, he had lost his every opportunity, supposing he ever had one with her, and married Miss Lucy Cotter.

He wondered if Lady Estcott knew that Lucy had been buried only six months ago. He thought that she did not, and that was just as well, for they were too old to worry about observing lengthy mourning. Admittedly, he was saddened on first seeing her, for she had seemed pale and ill, but after a few moment's conversation, his Elizabeth had come back.

He smiled in remembrance. He recalled the time Miss Adderly had turned suddenly and knocked the wig off the head of old Waddington, who was seated near her. She had shrieked and then laughed so hard she had fallen backward and would have gone into the punch bowl had he not caught her. Another time, Miss Adderly had stood in the garden at Chatsworth and vowed to dance with no one that evening if someone did not rescue a cat from a tree. No less than five gentlemen were attempting to ascend the tree at one time, while others came with chairs and poles and even a plow horse to stand upon. He forgot who it was now who finally saved the day by getting a stable lad who knew what he was about and had the cat down in a trice.

Miss Adderly's nickname had become "Kitten" from that day onward.

But years had passed . . . so many years. He was no longer the strapping soldier standing so proud in his dress uniform, and she was no longer that lively, exuberant young lady. But she most certainly did still have a mind of her own, he thought, and smiled once more.

He would love to spend the rest of his days with Lady Estcott . . . but he did not know if his luck would run any better this time than it had before. He had lost her to Etherington and then to Estcott; perhaps on this third and last chance, his luck would come home.

He came to his first stop of the morning, handed his rig over to his groom, and made his stiff-legged way up Lady Etherington's steps. He was let in, and found Lady Etherington and her granddaughter in her gold salon, entertaining two younger gentlemen and one older one. He bowed, and she smiled at him.

"It is about time you have come. I do not recall the last time I saw you in London for the season. I understand that your dear Lady Felstone is gone— let me offer my condolences."

He sat, slowly and carefully, and stretched his game leg out before him.

"She passed gently in her sleep. It is all I could wish for her."

"That is so true. I could not bear Etherington's suffering those last months. He was miserable, and it made me miserable, as well."

"He was yet a young man."

"I think that made it all the more grievous, yes. Thank the Lord my son does not have diabetes. It is an awful sickness."

"Miss Etherington," he said then, "you are not only as beautiful as your grandmother, but you dance as excellently as she. I congratulate you on your first evening at Almack's."

Miss Etherington smiled and thanked him. Then the other callers, impatient at waiting for him to complete his first sentiments, stepped into the conversation.

"She was the most beautiful young lady present," said one.

"Without a doubt," said another.

"And her grandmother was, without doubt, the star of them all."

Light laughter and smiles followed that, and the conversation continued on several different gambits until the first gentlemen began to take their leaves.

At last only Lord Felstone remained. He wished to rise himself, but did not want to be so rude as to leave too soon. Besides, his knee was aching abominably.

"Well, Lord Felstone, did you see the *Times*?" Lady Etherington asked.

"Yes, I did. I particularly recall what it said about you, Miss Etherington—'a young lady of superior grace, and surely one of the loveliest present.' "

"Thank you, sir."

"It *should* have said the *loveliest* present, but we must not refine upon it," said Lady Etherington.

"Indeed, no," said Felstone.

"But if you must know"—she glanced quickly at the door, although well aware they were alone—"I do wonder about Miss Marland. I know nothing about a Captain Marland, and I could learn not a thing about her mother. Well, that is not my concern, but one wonders if such a fuss would be made about her looks if the truth were to come out."

"The truth, Grandmother Etherington? What is it?"

"I do not know, and we must not speak of it. Do

you understand, my dear? We must not be parties to gossip."

"Of course not. I would never breathe a word."

Felstone took a deep breath. "Captain Marland was a navy man, and I am afraid I am not as well informed as I would otherwise be. I could certainly enquire into his record. But I am sure there is nothing to be found but what has been said."

"Likely so," said Lady Etherington. "And he is a relation of Lady Estcott, after all. It is Mrs. Marland who puzzles me the most. I am most astonished that Miss Marland was admitted to Almack's. The patronesses must know something that I do not." She gave a sharp little laugh.

Felstone had not seen this side of Lady Etherington before, not that he claimed a strong acquaintance with her. He found himself growing more and more uncomfortable, and not being a particular enthusiast of social machinations, he was becoming eager to take his leave . . . but for one thing. Lady Estcott needed him to be her ears.

"I do not suppose much will be discovered about Mrs. Marland, unless someone wishes to tell it."

"Exactly so," Lady Etherington said. "But who shall that someone be, I should like to know? Well, perhaps that person can be discovered. . . . I for one have never fallen back on my duties where propriety is concerned. If there is something to learn, I shall learn it."

Lord Felstone made his good-bye with considerable heaviness of heart. He very much feared that Lady Etherington would make an issue of this chink in Lady Estcott's armor, and he had the grievous duty of informing her of it.

Chapter Nine

*F*or the third morning in a row Georgiana came down to breakfast to find that Lady Estcott was not waiting for her. Her heart plummeted again, and she poured out her tea in lonely seclusion.

Lady Estcott was "ill" again. Since the day Lord Felstone called, she had stayed in bed with a headache, and they had not been home to callers nor had they returned any.

Georgiana knew that Lord Felstone had been the bearer of bad news, although she had not been allowed to hear it. It had to have been very bad indeed for Lady Estcott to avoid society for the last several days, considering her ambitions for Georgiana. Georgiana did not mind being least seen—in fact, she preferred it—but her concern for Lady Estcott demanded that she visit her and determine the cause of her despair.

Georgiana found Lady Estcott on her chaise, a damp cloth on her forehead, eyes closed, and as poor-tempered as the last time Georgiana had attempted to visit her during her dismals.

"I do not wish to visit," Lady Estcott snapped. "Take your good intentions and leave with them."

"But I need to speak to you, Lady Estcott."

"Whatever for? Can you not see that I am ill?"

"Yes, but it has been three days, and I am afraid it can wait no longer."

"What is so urgent that you must speak to me now?"

"Cook is complaining of mice."

"You cannot be annoying me on that head! Whatever is wrong with the silly woman? She knows what to do with mice."

"The coachman says one of the bays has gone lame."

"Does he expect me to go to the stable and rub liniment on its leg? Of all the—"

"The modiste has girls sick with the grippe, and our gowns cannot be fitted until Tuesday."

Lady Estcott cracked open her eyes and turned them pointedly to Georgiana. "You have made it all up, you wicked girl, and if you do not have a good explanation, I shall fling my vinaigrette at you, and then toss you from the drawing room window!"

"I am worried about what Lord Felstone may have

told you. I have not seen you so distraught since you could not get vouchers for me to attend Almack's."

Lady Estcott drew a breath and let it out heavily. "He told me nothing that you should worry about."

"I should like to know anyway."

"Perhaps it is none of your affair!" She glared at Georgiana, and then closed her eyes once more.

"If it is a private matter, I beg your pardon. But I do hope Lord Felstone is not ill."

"No, he is not ill. Everyone who is old is not ill. And it was not a 'private matter,' so do not think it." She paused for a long moment, and when she did not speak again, Georgiana did.

"Then it was about me."

"Stop speculating. It is nothing. It was only about some conceited person's curiosity. We cannot be thrown by things that—that have not happened."

Georgiana was silent a moment. Then she said, "I agree with you, Lady Estcott. But if there is something important, I should like to know, particularly if it is about me, so I may deal with it as I must. I should not want injury to extend any further than it should."

"You silly child." Lady Estcott sighed. "Does this mean you are all ready to return to that dreadful school, or somewhere like it? Do not be foolish. People shall think as they will, and their opinion of me shall be no less formed if you were to fly away somewhere. I am equal to it. I could not have lived so long if I were not."

"Then," Georgiana said softly, "come out of your room. It is a good deal more pleasant to be doing something."

She patted Lady Estcott's hand, then rose and left the room.

She did not have long to wait. That very afternoon Lady Estcott arose, dressed, and stated she wished to go driving. Georgiana quickly changed, and so did Miss Frey, who wished for an outing, as well. In a reasonable amount of time they entered the gates of Hyde Park. As it was late afternoon, the park was well populated with carriages, riders on horseback, and those on a fashionable stroll.

"I would love to walk," Georgiana said, gazing out the window.

She had no expectation that Lady Estcott or Miss Frey would wish to, but Miss Frey surprised her.

"I should like to, as well," she said.

"Then you shall," Lady Estcott responded. "Young ladies need exercise, as do ladies who are still young *enough*. As for me, I shall ride, for I am neither." She commanded the carriage to stop, and the younger ladies were let out.

"What a fine day!" Georgiana said. "I am so happy you came, Miss Frey, or I should have had to do nothing but ride, and I should soon become so fat that no one would know me."

Miss Frey smiled softly. "I thought you might like to walk."

"I think you are very clever, and I hope Lady Estcott knows how fortunate she is to have you."

"I am the fortunate one. I never awake without thinking how very lucky I have been in my life."

Georgiana fell silent then, thinking of Miss Frey's modesty and satisfaction with her lot in life, and knew that here was a lesson worth learning.

They walked for some time, enjoying the sights and sounds of the park in springtime, admiring the flowers, gazing at the elegant carriages, and studying the dress of the ladies who walked the path. The day was uncharacteristically sunny, and Georgiana felt that the brightness was meant to deliver a gift of hope.

"Oh, what is that?" She saw something tiny and brown moving in the grass and stepped off the path to investigate.

"Likely a mouse," said the practical Miss Frey, but she followed Georgiana.

Georgiana bent down. It was a baby bird, a fledgling yet unable to fly.

"Oh, poor thing. It should still be in his nest."

"He will make dinner for a very fortunate cat."

Georgiana carefully parted the grass around the bird and closed her hand around it. "I do believe you are funning with me. I am sure you like birds." Georgiana stood with the fragile parcel and looked at her friend's face. Miss Frey had a distinguishable twinkle in her eyes.

"Oh, I do like birds . . . particularly with currant jelly and a nice fresh dumpling."

"Well, this one will go home again. Do you see the nest?"

They gazed into the hawthorn hedge next to them. Georgiana hoped that the nest, should they find it, was not too deep in the shrub or there would be no way to avoid the thorns.

"I do believe that is it," said Miss Frey.

A small cup of dried grass was nestled in the branches, and Georgiana spotted the movement of another tiny brown head.

"Oh, dear. I shall tear my dress for certain."

"I daresay doing so in Hyde Park would not be the best plan."

Georgiana stared at the nest, looking for an angle whereby she might reach it and do the least harm, while Miss Frey waited patiently behind her.

"Good day, your lordship," said Miss Frey.

Georgiana straightened and turned around. There on the path were Lord Ryburn and Miss Etherington.

He looked at her and blinked; then he nodded. "Good day, Miss Marland. Miss Frey."

Miss Etherington stood beside him, smiling, her parasol perched on her shoulder. He glanced at Georgiana's cupped hands; Georgiana felt the heat rise in her face.

"I am on a mission of mercy, sir. This—this little thrush has fallen from his nest."

He stared at her. She stared back. And then he stepped off the path and approached her.

"Let me see."

She held up her hands and revealed the tiny bird. Its little black eyes stared up at Lord Ryburn's golden ones.

"The nest is in the hawthorn."

"Ah, yes. Of course it is in the hawthorn." He looked at her once more, and began removing his coat. "Give me the bird." He tossed the coat aside and pulled off one glove.

She carefully placed the fledgling in his big hand, and his fingers closed gently around it. He bent over then, stared into the thorny branches, and slowly reached in until the entire length of his arm was within the bush.

"Can you—?"

"One moment." He leaned in a bit more, and tucked the little bird into the nest. "Done."

"Oh, thank you. . . ."

Lord Ryburn was still slowly extricating himself from the hawthorn, so Georgiana waited to finish until he finally stood up.

"Thank you. We are fortunate you happened along."

Lord Ryburn was now engaged in brushing the leaves and twigs from his sleeves, but when he looked at her at last, there was a hint of a smile in his eyes.

"I am at your service anytime, Miss Marland," he said. Then he retrieved his jacket and his glove, and he and Miss Etherington were on their way down the path.

"He really is a fine gentleman," Miss Frey said, watching them walk away.

"Oh, no!"

Miss Frey looked at her in surprise. "Do you not agree?"

Georgiana did agree, but between the peril of the bird and the shock of seeing Lord Ryburn with Miss Etherington, she had completely forgotten about Lady Estcott. "Where is Lady Estcott?"

"Why, she has been driving around the park. Why do you ask?"

"I—I thought perhaps she might see Lord Ryburn."

"That would be very nice, I would think."

Of course it would. But Miss Frey, Georgiana realized, did not know of the animosity between Lady Estcott and Lady Etherington. "It is just that I think she would . . . rather see Lord Ryburn with Miss Hartley."

"I think you worry too much. Lady Estcott knows her great-nephew quite well. She will not be surprised."

When they returned to the carriage, Georgiana

learned that Lady Estcott had seen Lord Ryburn, but had not paused to chat. She did wonder what young lady he was walking with, she said, but her life was too short to dwell upon it.

Lady Estcott's plans for the party at her nephew Lord Wyndgrave's were complete and the invitations had been sent. When the day arrived, Lady Estcott decided that they were to stay the night and be comfortable, since the house was at the outskirts of town, had plenty of rooms, and the trip home was farther than she liked to travel late at night.

She wanted them to arrive very early, for she needed to supervise the decoration and did not like to be rushed. Consequently, the maids were required to pack their things and the footmen to load their traveling cases into the carriage. Done at last, they were on their way to Lord Wyndgrave's. Georgiana found herself looking forward to seeing Lord Ryburn, in spite of what good sense told her.

She had seen little of him since Almack's, although she did not precisely know why that concerned her. She knew he was looking for her mother, and certainly he was not required to give her more dancing lessons. Just as certainly, he was making good use of any time he had to spare, as her encounter with him in Hyde Park had proven.

She did know she had something to say to him as soon as she possibly could. Lord Ryburn needed to know about Lady Estcott and Lady Etherington before he had to learn it from Lady Estcott herself.

They were lucky in the weather again. It was warm enough to go out in only a light shawl, and when they arrived the sun was shining.

Georgiana gazed at the classical columns in front of Lord Wyndgrave's home and realized why Lady Estcott wanted to stay there that evening. The beautiful Italianate style, as well as the size of the home, was impressive indeed, and spoke well of the wealth of the owner, Lord Ryburn's father.

They were ushered inside. Georgiana stared in some wonder at the gilt and the marble cherubs in the front hall, at the marble underfoot, and the ornate plaster work and gilt framed mirrors.

"What is your opinion?" Lady Estcott asked.

"It—it looks like a palace."

"Hm. I suppose it does," was Lady Estcott's response. "My nephew is responsible for the cherubs. I am not partial to them. His father had more sense."

A deep laugh sounded, echoing off the walls and the marble floor and the cherubs and the mirrors, and a tall older gentleman, smiling broadly, stepped into view. "How lovely to see you, Aunt Estcott! The flowers have just been delivered. You are in time to see what is to be done with them. My house is yours—but pray do not put breeches on my cherubs!"

"Do not twit me, Richard, or it will not go well with you!"

"I should never do so. Come and have tea, and then you may supervise the flowers. The staff has started the ballroom—they cannot make many mistakes there, I think. Flowers on the columns, flowers on the balcony, etcetera, etcetera." He turned and led them through to the back of the house, with Georgiana and her aunt following.

The physical resemblance between Lord Wyndgrave and his son was all the more striking as Lord Wyndgrave was a very fit gentleman for his age. He walked with an easy stride and an upright bearing, but there was a definite jauntiness to his attitude that she missed in his son.

"This way, ladies. We are enjoying the terrace while the sun is yet with us."

He stepped out through wide doors onto the terrace, a broad covered porch separated from the garden by an impressive colonnade.

"Corinthian," he said cheerfully, pointing at the columns. "Do you know your ancient Greek history, my dear?" He glanced back at Georgiana, still smiling.

"A little. I believe the Greeks did not make so much in the Corinthian style."

She heard a soft chuckle, and looked to her left. Lord Ryburn, holding a glass of wine, was seated a stone's throw away at a cloth-covered table. On the table was another glass, ostensibly his father's.

"I understand her school teaches a range of subjects," said Lord Ryburn. He rose to his feet. "Good afternoon, Aunt Estcott. Miss Marland."

"Good afternoon. Your father has promised me tea."

They sat down at the table. It was cool on the shaded terrace, and Georgiana pulled her shawl more closely around her.

"I think Miss Marland would take some tea, as well." Lord Wyndgrave rang the bell, and a footman immediately appeared from inside the doorway. "Tea for the ladies."

The footman vanished, and Lord Wyndgrave looked back at Georgiana. "My son was quite right," he said. "You are an exceptionally beautiful young lady."

Georgiana felt herself blush, a trait she heartily disliked in herself.

"Richard, do not flirt with Miss Marland," said Lady Estcott.

"What? Do you say I flirt?" Lord Wyndgrave asked with such an expression of incredulity that Georgiana smiled.

"Is the king an Englishman?"

"You cut me to the quick, dear Aunt. I was merely admiring the young lady, and expressing my appreciation in a gentlemanly fashion."

"I thank you, sir," said Lord Ryburn, "for drawing Aunt Estcott's attention from *me*. Perhaps she might look about to find you a wife, as well."

"My dear boy, had I known twenty-seven years ago what I do now, I should have wept myself into an early grave. How can you even jest about such a thing?"

"Aunt, he is clearly a lonely man. There must be something you can do."

Lord Wyndgrave laughed. "I surrender! Here is the tea. Let us speak on a more *innocent* subject, shall we?"

During this exchange, Georgiana noticed something: Lord Ryburn was smiling. There was a rapport between father and son, as much as they were different from each other. She also thought about what Lord Wyndgrave had said: that Lord Ryburn had called her beautiful. She did not know whether she should take it to heart, but it affected her, nonetheless.

For a while afterward it was just pleasantness, with small talk, the cool breeze, and the scent of flowers. Georgiana's gaze strayed over the garden, where the sun still shone, although a haze had begun to come in.

"Perhaps you would like to look at the garden," Lord Ryburn said.

She glanced at him in surprise and gratitude. "I should like that very much."

They arose and descended the shallow steps into the garden, where Georgiana gloried in the touch of the sun. The garden was formal, with sunken beds divided by walks and an elaborate fountain in the center. They began by walking the outer path.

"I wanted to explain—"

"I wanted to tell you—"

They both paused and looked at each other. Lord Ryburn smiled and Georgiana laughed.

"What did you wish to tell me?" Lord Ryburn asked.

Her courage faltered, and she looked away. "I am afraid I will sound ridiculous."

"That is not unusual in my family. Pray, tell me."

She glanced at his face and saw that he was yet smiling, and there was sincerity in his eyes.

"You will think it forward of me and think me a busybody. But—" She glanced back at the colonnaded terrace, and saw that aunt and nephew were in conversation, and distant enough not to overhear.

"It is a secret, and not mine to tell, but I feel I must, for your sake as well as your aunt's."

"My aunt's?" He suddenly looked concerned, and his smile vanished.

Georgiana swallowed. "Let us walk."

They continued on past the carefully tended bed of daffodils and tulips. Georgiana sought to gain her composure and slow her racing heart. At last she took a breath and began. "Long ago there was a rivalry between your aunt and Lady Etherington."

"Ah. Now, I see."

"Do you?" She glanced at him once more as they walked, and he gave her a rueful smile.

"Absolutely. You do not need to reveal so very much of the secret, you see. You are going to tell me that she would not be happy that I have been in company with Lady Etherington's granddaughter."

"I only wanted you to understand the situation. I should never suggest what you should do."

"And I should not expect you to."

They walked farther in silence. Georgiana felt a great relief, and yet it seemed that her task had been a good deal too easy.

"I, on the other hand," he said presently, "meant to ask you not to refine too much on my appearance with Miss Etherington. We are not well acquainted."

"You do not owe me any explanation."

"No, but I wish to give it. You see, Miss Hartley will attend tonight . . . as well as Miss Etherington. I did not want to cause you any confusion or undue concern."

"Oh! Oh . . . dear. Now I am afraid that I *am* concerned!"

"Yes, but I did not realize the detail about Aunt Estcott and Lady Etherington. I only felt it appropriate that Lady Etherington and her granddaughter be invited."

"Then Lady Estcott knows."

"Aunt Estcott does *not* know. My father also sent invitations."

"Well . . . I hope the seating arrangements may be altered at dinner!"

"The Etheringtons are not dinner guests, thank the Lord."

They continued to stroll along the path. Privately, Georgiana was feeling a happiness she had not expected. Lord Ryburn had actually felt he must explain Miss Etherington to her! It did not matter what reason he gave for telling her; it only mattered that he had felt it necessary.

There was a deep border of trees, rather like a small forest, on the outside perimeter of the garden, and Georgiana felt a restfulness as she gazed into it.

"I should so love to walk in the trees."

"Then we shall." He took her arm and stepped between two bordering trees.

"I am afraid I am not shod for this."

"We need not go far."

Instead, they paused beneath the shelter of the branches of a great oak and gazed into the dappled light and shadow. A squirrel darted and scrambled up a tree; they heard the sweet *switt-witt-witt* of a goldfinch, and Georgiana spotted it in the lower branches of a gooseberry bush.

He drew a breath. "There is something else I wish to tell you."

"What is it?" She felt slightly alarmed when she looked at him, for he appeared very solemn.

"It is about your mother," he said.

Her heart thudded heavily, then fell to the soles of her feet.

Chapter Ten

"I have not been able to find your mother nor any news of her." Hugh paused, but she made no answer. She only stared at him, and he felt the painful impact of his words upon her.

"I have had my man search as many parish records as he could in the London area for evidence of her marriage or death, but he has found nothing. Of course, that does not mean a record does not exist, only that we have not found it. And if no such record exists, that may not signify, either. People can vanish without a trace. They can die and their names never be discovered; they can meet foul play and not be found; they can change their names and go where no one will recognize them."

Hugh hesitated, watching her face. The dappled light that had brightened it earlier was fading away, but he still thought he saw a glimmer of tears. He hated this so very, very much.

"I would need to locate someone who knows her and has had some recent contact with her to find her. An old man who lives near your mother's last address does remember a woman who fits her description, but he did not know her name or where she went. The other neighbors have changed since three years past."

She lowered her gaze. "Then it is hopeless."

"Perhaps. Perhaps not. But I think we may consider that your mother may not wish to be found."

"But why? Why would she . . ." Miss Marland stopped speaking, as if she knew her own answer.

"Why would she not be in touch with you? She may wish to protect you. She may not want you to know her current circumstances."

Miss Marland did not respond.

"Another reason one disappears is, of course, to escape debt. And the need of money can force someone to a way of life they never wished for."

"I realize all of those things," Miss Marland said rather sharply. He heard her sniff. "But I still wish to find her, no matter what may be the case." Then she added more quietly, "If she is alive . . ."

Hugh thought guiltily of the woman at Miss Silby's Academy but kept the secret. He had no more reason to believe the woman than to disbelieve her; it was as likely as not she made up a story to earn two crown.

"Let us not forget," he said gently, "that learning nothing is not necessarily a bad thing. What we cannot discover others are unlikely to learn. If your mother's affairs are best kept hidden, matters could be a deal worse than this."

"I should like to know if she is dead . . . or not." She was looking off into the distance again, seemingly at a woodpecker creeping along the trunk of an old elm. "That is enough. I should be satisfied with that."

He felt for her. He did not know when, but he had lost the nagging suspicion that she knew something about her mother that she had not shared. He had also at some point lost that irksome feeling that she had somehow placed herself in his aunt's life to upset his, even though he had nearly always known that was not true.

He also recognized in her a lonely person, a young one at that, trying to find her way and steadfastly trying to do the best she could. And he saw a young woman with a kind heart who would save a baby bird and cajole his sometimes-cranky aunt out of her moods. He knew she did this, for his aunt liked her, and the spark was back in the old lady's eyes.

He was not certain, however, as to when he had started having thoughts of taking her in his arms and kissing her.

"We had best go back," he said.

There came a pattering sound overhead, and a cold drop fell on his nose.

She looked at him, and he realized he could no longer see her face.

"It is raining," she said.

"Thank you. So I observe."

"It is pleasant here under the oaks, listening to the rain on the leaves. You can look up at the sky and not get a drop on your face."

"My dear, there you are wrong. You can look up, but I promise you, you *will* get a drop on your face."

There was a moment of silence, but he knew she was looking at him.

"I challenge you," she said.

"You wish to challenge me? To look up?"

"Yes."

He did not recall doing anything this foolish since he had been a child, but he looked up. So did she. They stood there in the deep shadow under the trees and looked up at the gray, angry sky past the tree-tops.

A drop smacked him in the eye.

"It is done. I win," he said. "I have the wet face to prove it."

She laughed lightly. He liked her laugh; he liked to hear her laugh when he knew he had caused her tears only moments before. Perhaps she was only pretending her spirits were better, but for now he could not know the truth of it.

"We need to go. The rain will likely come down harder rather than stop, and then where will we be?"

"Under these trees," she said. "But I suppose we should go. Even Lady Estcott and Lord Wyndgrave will begin to wonder what happened to us."

"True, and the evening will be interesting enough as it is."

The servants and the staff from the florist had done wonders in a short period of time. Floral bouquets and white and gold ribbons had gone up everywhere, even decorating the stair banisters; Georgiana noticed this on her way upstairs after dinner.

"It is beautiful, Lady Estcott."

Lady Estcott, who was climbing the stairs in front of her, answered, "It came out rather well. Fortunately, my nephew hired people who knew what they were about. It is a good thing he took my advice."

They reached the top and traversed the hall to their assigned rooms.

"Agnes will come to you when she is finished with me," Lady Estcott said. "You may look about now for a bit if you like, but be sure to be in your room by half past the hour."

"Yes. I shall."

Lady Estcott entered her room and closed the door behind her, and Georgiana looked down the empty hallway, wondering where she might find the gallery. At that moment, Lord Ryburn came out of a room a short way down the hall and saw her.

"Miss Marland—I do not suppose you are lost."

"Oh, no. But I have some minutes to spare. Lady Estcott said that your father has a gallery, and I was just wondering where it is."

"I shall take you there."

"I do not wish to be any trouble."

"It is no trouble at all." He walked up to her, took her arm, and led her to the stairs going up to the next floor.

"You are being very kind, Lord Ryburn. I thank you." She watched her feet as they climbed, so she felt rather than saw his expression.

"How odd that you should thank me for something I should always have been. I am quite rightly chastised."

She glanced up at him. "But I never meant to chastise you!"

"Of course you did not. But the fact remains that I have not always behaved so well toward you. Noting any kindness on my part now serves to remind me that it is an unusual event."

He did not appear to be jesting, and she looked away, uncertain how to reply. "Please, think nothing of it."

"And now I am being unkind again. Perhaps I cannot be cured. Possibly you may help me by suggesting a new topic of conversation?"

Now she heard the lightness in his voice once more. She smiled at him as they reached the top of the stairs. "Perhaps. I shall begin by asking that you introduce me to all of your ancestors."

"To some of them I shall. Only the ones whom I like."

They walked slowly down the gallery, pausing to look at portraits of various ancestors, and here and there among those a landscape. Finally they reached a portrait of Lord Wyndgrave as a young man, and Georgiana gazed at it for a long time. "You might be able to convince me that he is you, disguised in old style dress."

"I am afraid he is not—but it is amusing to think that this was made of me at a costume ball."

"And yet, you and your father are so different."

They moved on to the next portrait—that of a lovely young woman—but this was a carefully rendered sketch rather than a painting.

"Who is this?"

"It is my mother. But the next is a proper portrait of her."

Next to the sketch was a painting of the same lovely woman. Georgiana looked at it, and then went back to the sketch. "This is better," she said. "She looks more alive—almost as if she is about to speak."

"That is how I wished her to look."

She glanced at him questioningly.

"It is a drawing I made of her from memory. She died when I was very young."

He was gazing not at her, but at the sketch as he

spoke, but she read much in his look. "I am sorry for your loss. It seems I have been thinking only of myself, and talking to you of my mother, when you have lost your own."

"It was a long time ago. I was seven years old when she died."

"Then it must have been very hard for you. You were so young when you lost her." Sensing he was reluctant to respond, she continued, "The drawing is truly very good. Have you drawn other subjects?"

"Yes . . . but not recently. The subject must be something I value."

"Something you wish to preserve."

"No, it is only the likeness you preserve. But that is the only thing you truly can keep. All of these ancestors"—he waved his hand—"are gone, but their likenesses will last much longer."

Georgiana felt inexplicably sad. There was something more in his words, something she could not quite grasp. He was telling her something he truly believed about life. But as she looked at him, and as they turned away from the portrait, she knew she would not learn the answer then. She must go to change for the evening ahead.

Lady Estcott was furious when she learned that Lady Etherington and her daughter would attend, but after some private moments to recover from the knowledge that those ladies were coming, she presented her usual composed face when the guests began to arrive. She even managed a civil greeting to her foe, which Georgiana, standing at Lady Estcott's side greeting arrivals, was able to witness.

Georgiana was glad to see the arrival of Lord Felstone. Observing covertly, she noticed Lady Estcott brighten as she greeted him, although the subtle relief in her attitude was such that only someone who was very familiar with her would notice it.

Tonight Georgiana wore white muslin worked with silver over blue silk. She thought she looked very well, but soon the arrival of the other ladies caused her to revise her opinion to "well enough." Miss Etherington arrived in a beautiful gown of pale blue muslin over white satin, the blue overdress trimmed with exquisite lace and her pale shoulders exposed as much as possible for fashion. Georgiana had to admit that Miss Etherington had every right to suppose that she was the most beautiful young lady in attendance.

The arrival of Miss Hartley was of equal interest to Georgiana. Miss Hartley was a tall, slender brunette. She wore green silk to great advantage, and she could claim the most poise. She attended with her mother, and presented herself with a queenliness that Georgiana felt she could never acquire.

Some time later, as they stood in the green salon where the guests initially gathered, Lady Estcott indicated Miss Hartley with a nod. "That is the young woman you should model yourself upon," she said. "In manners and bearing there is no one better."

Knowing that Miss Hartley was Lord Ryburn's first choice made Georgiana even more regretful that she could not attain this lofty goal of perfection, but she assented to Lady Estcott's suggestion. As she gazed at Miss Hartley, Lord Ryburn walked up to the young woman and her mother. At that moment Lady Estcott summoned Georgiana in a different direction. They went from guest to guest as Lady Estcott did her duty as hostess and made certain that Georgiana was properly known to them. Then, the first portion of the entertainment was to begin.

Lady Estcott called the group to attention in her most regal tone. "Ladies and gentlemen, if you would be seated, I have asked Miss Marland to play the pianoforte. I would like all the young ladies who wish to perform to take a turn, as well."

Georgiana felt nearly immobile with fear. She walked to the pianoforte and pulled off her gloves. Her hands were clammy; she rubbed them together and stared at the keyboard. She became aware of a figure standing near her, and she glanced up to see Lord Ryburn.

"Allow me to turn your pages," he said quietly. There was a world of understanding in his eyes, and she felt herself begin to relax.

"Thank you, sir."

She began. She felt that she faltered at first, but

then her fingers warmed to the task and she gave her heart to the music, her favorite Haydn.

As she played, she was only vaguely aware of Lord Ryburn turning the pages; his timing was perfectly in tune with her and did nothing to draw her attention. Finally, she became completely unaware of him, and knew only the beautiful world that she inhabited while playing Haydn.

The last trills sounded and her fingers stilled. There was the briefest silence—and then enthusiastic applause.

Georgiana stood, mildly dazed from her performance, and gave a curtsy. Then Lord Ryburn took her arm and led her back to her seat next to Lady Estcott.

"That was lovely," he whispered into her ear. Then he stepped away, taking some of her happiness with him.

Other performances followed. Miss Etherington sang very sweetly and to great applause, while Miss Hartley played the harp. Several others also performed, including two sisters who sang a duet. When the program came to a close, the guests followed Lady Estcott to the ballroom where the musicians were preparing for an evening of dancing.

The ballroom was impressive, as were the other rooms in Lord Wyndgrave's home. It was much smaller and more intimate than the ballroom at Almack's, but Georgiana thought that made it all the nicer.

Roses and ribbons decorated all of the columns

and the front of the musician's balcony, as Lord Wyndgrave had mentioned. Fresh candles were in place, and in the salon across from the ballroom there was a table laden with drinks, cold meats, quail, bread, jam, fruit tarts, sweetmeats, and more.

Seating was arranged around the sides of the room, separated from the dancing area by colonnades. Georgiana sat with Lady Estcott, some distance from the Etheringtons. She was, however, close to Miss Hartley and her mother, Lady Hartley, with whom Lady Estcott was engaged in conversation.

Georgiana was engaged in gazing upward at the elaborately painted ceiling when she heard her name spoken.

"Miss Marland, I hope you will give me your first dance."

She looked up to see Lord Ryburn standing there smiling, and her heart turned over. "I should be happy to."

"My father wished to steal you from me for your first dance, but I was able to convince him otherwise." His eyes twinkled, and he extended his hand. She took it, and he assisted her from her chair to the dance floor where the others were gathering.

It was the most wonderful dance Georgiana had ever experienced. Lord Ryburn was her partner at last—not as her instructor in Lady Estcott's drawing room, but at a ball. She did not care anymore about the other ladies' gowns. She did not care that she was simply Miss Marland, whose fate was inclined to change. Now she was Lord Ryburn's chosen partner, and that was all that mattered in the world.

When she met him in the dance and he took her hand with a smile, this time she knew it all was truly for her, and not for reassurance. How foolish it was for her to enjoy this so much, but she would, and every moment.

The half hour ended much too soon. Lord Ryburn returned her to Lady Estcott. Soon she was approached by another gentleman, but when she saw Lord Ryburn lead out his Miss Hartley, her feet suddenly felt firmly attached to the floor.

It was after this dance that Miss Hartley spoke with her as they stood by the refreshment table.

"I quite approve of your gown," said Miss Hartley. "It is very lovely."

"Thank you, although I must give Lady Estcott all the credit for it."

"Yes, she is an estimable lady with excellent taste. With her assistance, you cannot go wrong." She sipped her lemonade and then said, "Have you met a gentleman of interest?"

Georgiana felt this question was a very forward one, especially coming from the impeccable Miss Hartley, but she answered it. "No, I have not. I expect Lady Estcott will guide me. I owe everything to her kindness, and I trust in her wisdom."

"Excellently said. Your position is an unusual one

after all, and were it mine, I should wish for such assistance. Mine, of course, is rather different. I do not say that in pride—it is every bit as difficult in a different way." Her gaze strayed to the other guests in the refreshment salon and apparently found no one else of interest, as she looked back at Georgiana.

"I am very nearly engaged," she said. "In our circle, some things can happen rapidly; others are abominably slow. But I do expect that Lord Ryburn will propose very soon. We are exceptionally well suited, and our families are in agreement."

Georgiana forced a smile. "A fine match, indeed. I wish you well."

Georgiana was not sorry when the conversation ended. She suspected that Miss Hartley's purpose for it, in retrospect, was to be certain Georgiana knew where she stood, both in society and with Lord Ryburn.

She left the refreshment salon shortly after Miss Hartley, crossed to the open double doors to the ballroom, and immediately knew she could not return to dancing—not yet. She needed to organize her thoughts, establish a course to follow, and no longer allow herself to be blown about by the whims of her heart.

Lord Ryburn might like her very well, but he would never marry her. Indeed, he *could* not, unless he were much more reckless than she knew him to be.

She turned away from all of the beauty and light in the ballroom and followed the hall to the stairs. She descended slowly, alone, her destination the terrace where she would gain the peace she needed.

When she stepped out upon the terrace, she was very glad to have her shawl. The rain had stopped some hours ago, but it was a cool night—cool and starless. There was a moon, however, that cast a thin light between the clouds. She gazed up at it, and the unwanted memory came, of Lord Ryburn and herself beneath the oaks, looking up at the rainy sky.

I could love you, Lord Ryburn, but I shall not. You have your place, and I have mine—although I do not wholly know where mine is. Oh, I wish Lady Estcott had not made me her heiress. I wish she had not thought to try to make me something I am not. I wish I was back at Miss Silby's, teaching lessons and caring for the girls. And I wish you all the good fortune in the world, and I hope you find love.

She stared at the slice of moon as it ducked behind a traveling cloud and peeked out again, and she felt dampness on her face that was not rain.

She heard a sudden sound.

She blinked and brought herself back to the present. She heard something that was not the faint sound of music coming from the ballroom. It reminded her of the mewing of a kitten, but she suspected it was not. Then, she saw the movement of something white on the verge of the garden.

Georgiana descended the terrace steps and approached the place where she had seen the flash of white, following the grayish walk in the faint light of the moon. She stepped past the shadow of a tree and saw them.

A gentleman carrying a woman in his arms was coming toward her. She could not identify them in the dark, but she stood and waited for their approach, sensing that they might need her help.

"Is there something I may do?" she asked.

"Miss Marland." The voice sounded relieved. It was Lord Ryburn's. "Miss Etherington had a small accident, and I should very much appreciate your help."

A mix of feelings came over Georgiana—shock, concern, and gratitude that she was needed.

"I am sorry," whispered a small voice.

Georgiana turned to walk beside them. "It is all right, Miss Etherington. I am here, and I shall guarantee your safety."

A pause. "Thank you." And then Miss Etherington began to weep.

"We only meant to have a private conversation," Lord Ryburn said. "I did not intend this to happen."

"It was my fault," Miss Etherington wailed. "I ran away."

"She turned her ankle."

"Are you in pain, Miss Etherington?" Georgiana asked.

"Yes," she said softly. "It hurts. I was not supposed to *truly* injure myself."

Georgiana glanced at Lord Ryburn, but he said nothing. She looked back at Miss Etherington. "It is only important now that you are safe and I am here. I have been with you all the time and saw you fall on the steps. Is that how it happened?"

The girl's pause gave Georgiana a moment's concern, but then she answered. "Yes. Please. Grandmama will be unhappy, but I do not care."

"Lady Etherington will be unhappy that you are saved from scandal?"

"Do not ask," Lord Ryburn said dryly.

"Yes." Miss Etherington began to weep again.

"I believe she has sprained her ankle. She lost her footing on the walk while running. I shall carry her upstairs, and if you would be so kind as to remain with us—"

"Of course."

They reached the terrace, entered the house, then climbed the stairs. When they reached the ballroom floor, several guests standing in the hall between the ballroom and the salon saw them.

"Please summon Lady Etherington," Lord Ryburn said and continued up the stairs.

He carried Miss Etherington into one of the rooms and laid her on the bed. Lady Etherington entered almost immediately, and when she saw Georgiana, she glared at her. "What have you to do with this?" she demanded.

"Why, nothing, except that I was accompanying Miss Etherington."

"Miss Etherington, Miss Marland, and I stepped out for air," Lord Ryburn said. "Unfortunately, Miss Etherington fell and injured herself."

"I do not believe it!" Lady Etherington came to her granddaughter's bedside. "Is this true?"

Miss Etherington quailed and gulped. Georgiana held her breath.

"Yes, Grandmama, it is. I fell on the steps."

Georgiana reached for the bell to call for a maid, hoping she would arrive before Lady Etherington could release too much anger on the poor girl.

"I shall summon a doctor," Lord Ryburn said.

"Nonsense," snapped Lady Etherington. "Caroline, show *me* your injury."

Lord Ryburn waited at the door, knowing as Georgiana did that Lady Etherington would discover the injury to be real.

"Yes, I would rather that you call the doctor," said Lady Etherington at last, discouragement plain in her voice. "I believe it is only a sprain, but she must have the best of care."

"Of course. I shall do so immediately."

Georgiana followed Lord Ryburn out the door, certain that nothing worse could happen that night.

Chapter Eleven

*L*ord Ryburn stopped Georgiana once they had gone a distance down the hall toward the stairs. He clasped her hand and said, "Thank you. I shall never be able to repay you for what you just did."

Georgiana searched his clear golden eyes and saw sincerity and warmth. Yet he wore a slight frown.

"You may thank fate, as well, for that is what was responsible for my being on the terrace just then." She hesitated and thought: *fate, and Miss Hartley.*

"Then I also thank fate." He sighed. "I wish you to know that I meant only to explain to Miss Etherington that the feelings of her grandmother and my great-aunt made any further attention on my part unadvisable. I should have been more cautious—it was her preference to go to the terrace to speak. But she became overwrought and ran down the steps into the garden, and I could do nothing but go after her."

"Lord Ryburn," Georgiana said gently, "again, you do not need to explain."

"But I must."

"No, you need not. I understand what happened. Her grandmother compelled her to do as she did—only it seems she was to pretend her injury."

Lord Ryburn uttered something completely ungentlemanly and then caught himself. "Forgive me. I am dreadfully sorry. I do not—"

"You are as overwrought as Miss Etherington is. It is clear that she did not wish to entrap you, you know. She was very glad to be rescued."

He sighed again. "Yes, I know."

"I imagine there is another gentleman who has caught her fancy."

He smiled weakly. "I for once should be grateful not to be flattered."

She smiled back at him, and they walked toward the stairs once more.

"The devil of it is that I still have some explanations to give. But as long as I can say that you were with us, all should be forgiven."

"I am certain that it will."

Georgiana thought then of Miss Hartley's confidence that his proposal was forthcoming and told herself that she was happy to have saved him—if only she had saved him for someone he could love.

The music had stopped by the time they reached the ballroom. People approached them from all sides—everyone wanted to learn what had happened and how badly Miss Etherington was injured. Georgiana played her role to good effect, and soon she was rewarded with murmurs of sympathy for the poor girl and nothing more.

Lord Wyndgrave, for his part, was loud in his sympathies and surprisingly jovial. He slapped his son on the back and said, "My son, a hero—saving the damsel in distress. But I beg the rest of you young ladies to stay indoors for the remainder of the evening. My son must recover from the effects of his chivalry."

It was Lady Estcott who was happiest, however. She took Georgiana by the arm and conducted her to her chair, where she told her that she was very glad that Lord Ryburn had sense enough not to be with Miss Etherington alone, and that Georgiana had been willing to accompany them.

"You must sit and rest now. Your hem is damp, too. In any event, our special guest is about to arrive."

"Special guest?"

"Yes. It is to be a surprise, but I shall tell you, for I think you have had enough of surprises for one evening. My nephew has engaged Miss Gloriane Garson of Covent Garden to perform tonight. We have not yet been to the opera, or you would know her. She has the most beautiful voice ever heard."

Georgiana waited patiently. Her only thought was that after Miss Garson performed, she would be able to retire for the evening. Her relief lasted only until the lady was introduced.

Beaming, Lord Wyndgrave stood up with the lady on the dais on one end of the ballroom. "And now, ladies and gentlemen, I am very pleased to present to you a surprise—Miss Gloriane Garson!"

Georgiana stared. For the briefest moment she thought she was mistaken, but then, she knew.

Gloriane Garson was none other than one Mrs. Marland, her mother.

Lord Ryburn gazed at the beautiful Gloriane Garson with appreciation. He knew her appearance and voice well from the performances he had attended, and she never failed to please him.

Gloriane was not a young woman, but she was not so very old, either. She was older than he, and younger than his father, he guessed—and fate had been kind to her face and her voice.

Gloriane had thick blond hair swept into an elaborate up-do, and she was a buxom lady, although she did not display herself as some lady performers did. Her gown was striking, a golden shade of satin elaborately embroidered and sewn with paste jewels, but her neckline was modest. In contrast to that, however, were the paint and rouge she used, however light.

She smiled beautifully, and her eyes swept over the gathering. Then she nodded to the musicians, and the strains of a violin began. In a moment, Gloriane's sweet, full voice filled the ballroom.

Hugh chose that moment to look over at where Miss Marland was sitting to see how she was enjoying the performance. To his shock, he saw her staring dumbly at Gloriane Garson—and Georgiana's face was chalk white.

Damme. He rose and began to make his way toward her; but suddenly, she was on her feet, hurrying quickly for the door.

Hugh moved as rapidly as he could without creating a spectacle, but by the time he reached the hall she was out of sight. He glanced quickly into the refreshment salon, only to find it empty; then he took the stairs and went straight to her room.

He knocked on her door, but heard not a sound from within.

"Miss Marland, it is I." He waited. Still there was nothing. Unsatisfied, he made the bold move of trying her door. It was not locked, so he pushed it open.

The room was empty.

He stood there, baffled, running over in his mind the various places she might go; only one suggested itself as practical. She had gone back to the terrace, a place she knew and where she would expect to see no one.

He quickly hurried down the two flights of stairs and stepped out onto the terrace.

He did not see her at first, but then his eyes adjusted to the darkness. She stood at the far end, staring out across the garden, as a new, gentle rain pattered lightly on the roof.

He approached her slowly until he came to stand beside her. She clutched her shawl around her, and she was shivering. Wordlessly he took off his coat and placed it around her shoulders.

"Gloriane Garson is your mother," he said gently.

She did not respond; she only gulped back a faint sob.

"My dear, it is not the end of everything. She is alive, and she is doing something of value to everyone who hears her, because she is a remarkable singer."

Georgiana swallowed again. "She is . . . an opera singer."

"Yes."

"I know . . . I should be happy . . . and I am, but . . . now, I must leave."

"Leave? And go where? Back to Miss Silby's? I am afraid you cannot."

"I know. She cannot afford an additional teacher.

And . . . if I am involved in scandal . . . she could not have me, in any case. I am not certain who would . . . but I shall have to go somewhere."

A grief gripped him that he had not felt for a long, long time. He remained silent for a moment while he dealt with it and then he spoke again.

"I cannot let you go in that way. You would not be safe. I will not have you accepting any employment just to remove yourself from my aunt's home. And, I must add, you need go nowhere unless she requests it of you."

"She will."

"No one but us knows that Gloriane Garson is your mother, and I do only because I saw how you looked at her. No one else will so much as conceive of it."

She sniffed and hung her head.

"Miss Marland, there is nothing to do but wait and see. If anything unfortunate should happen, I shall be the one to assist you. I insist upon it. You must promise me that you will do nothing rash before speaking to me."

"I—I cannot burden you that way."

"I am asking you to."

"You wish to marry Miss Hartley. I—I must not endanger your future any more than I—already have."

"The choice of what I do and will not do is mine. Do not try to choose for me."

She sniffed again, and then he turned her toward

him and took her in his arms. She folded against his breast the way that the little fledgling bird she had saved had snuggled back into its nest.

They stood there together for some time, listening to the gentle patter of the rain in the darkness. Then, regretfully, Lord Ryburn stepped back and gently escorted her inside.

Gloriane Garson left immediately after her performance. There was no opportunity for Georgiana to speak with her, even if it had been safe, and so Georgiana went to bed that night at Lord Wyndgrave's with her devastation complete.

I lose everyone I love. She could not even attempt to reason with herself tonight, for her discouraging thoughts were proving to be amazingly true. Her mother had abandoned her, Lord Ryburn would soon be lost to her, and even Lady Estcott, whom she had learned to love for all of her demanding ways, would probably turn her back on her.

Georgiana was too weary to pass another sleepless night, and much too soon she awoke to remembered pain. She made a resolution as she dressed for breakfast: Come what may, she was going to see her mother.

They arrived back on Park Lane in the afternoon, and the remainder of the day was quiet. Lord Felstone called the next morning, much to the delight of Lady Estcott.

Lord Felstone sat with them for longer than the prescribed half hour, and then, as he was on the point of leaving, he made a proposal.

"I have been thinking that it would be a very fine thing to attend the opera. Would you ladies agree to be my guests? We may hear Miss Garson perform again."

Lady Estcott, knowing nothing of Gloriane Garson's identity, immediately agreed. For Georgiana's part, she was very thankful to Lord Felstone for forming the plan.

"I shall ask Hugh to attend. He would be a comfortable escort for you, would he not, dear?"

Comfortable? No, that certainly would not be the case. In fact, he was the last person Georgiana wanted to accompany her on this venture. But Lady Estcott's mind was made up, so the plan was set for the very next evening Gloriane Garson was to perform.

They arrived at the Theatre Royal, Covent Garden, on a cool evening. Relations seemed similarly cool between Lord Ryburn and Georgiana, for neither of them had much to say to the other. It was due to the weight of the secret on his part, Georgiana thought, and the weight of *another* secret on her own part.

In spite of attending the theater infrequently, Lady Estcott maintained a box, and it was there that they sat. Georgiana anxiously awaited the presentation of her mother, for she would see the full performance for the first time, and without the fear that her mother would see *her*.

Her mother's portion of the program was early in the evening, for which Georgiana was grateful. Her plan would be difficult enough with the bad luck in the form of Lord Ryburn seated beside her.

Then her mother started to sing. Georgiana watched, and then, with her eyes closed, listened to the voice she had known all of her life, pushing the way her mother looked tonight from her thoughts and remembering her as she had been: a slender dark-haired woman with porcelain skin that had never felt the touch of paint. She dreaded the end of the performance, both for the loss of the music and from her fear of what was to come.

And then, the time came.

It was the interval between performances when one could stand and move about, and Georgiana quickly rose. She was soon to learn, however, that Lord Ryburn was not about to allow her to go anywhere alone. Even when she used the excuse of visiting the ladies' room, Lord Ryburn arranged for Lady Estcott to accompany her. She was distraught when the time came to return to their box without her having had the least opportunity of escape.

She waited through another performance, this of a gentleman she neither knew nor cared about. When the time came to rise again, she was resolved to be bold.

She refused to wait for Lady Estcott. There was nothing Lady Estcott could do, being incapable of keeping up with her, and thus Georgiana made her escape.

Holding her skirt aloft to keep it from being stepped on, she found herself nudged this way and that by various gentlemen and ladies walking to and from the boxes. At one point, she saw a gentleman she was acquainted with and quickly averted her face, her heart pounding. Then she at last found herself in the passage to the performer's rooms.

She nearly collided with a gentleman, and when she looked up she beheld the last performer, who stared at her with interest.

"I am looking for Gloriane Garson."

He hesitated, but only briefly, before pointing out the correct door. She hurried past him and then stopped at the door. At first she could not compel herself to raise her hand, but she found the courage to knock.

"Who is it?"

Georgiana took a breath. "It is Miss Marland."

The long hesitation from within nearly dashed her hopes, but then the door opened slightly, and her mother looked out. She gazed at Georgiana for a moment that seemed to last much longer; then she quickly stepped back. "Come in."

Georgiana stepped inside, and her mother quickly closed the door behind her.

"You should not have come," her mother said. She sat at her dressing table and began patting powder on her face.

"I had to come." Georgiana's breath was coming jaggedly, and for the first time in her life she felt she must pass out.

"It can do you great harm, and I do not wish for that." Her mother looked at her, and suddenly rose. "Sit down."

"No, I—"

"Quickly. Sit down, *now*." Her mother rapidly drew forth a chair, and pressed Georgiana into it. "I cannot have you fainting in here. Where is your escort? Why are you alone?"

Georgiana blinked back tears. "I only wanted to see you again . . . Mother." She started to weep. Her mother sighed, and then bent down and wrapped her arms around her.

"There you are, Angel Face. It is all right. Do not cry. You will get your mother's costume all wet."

"Why—why did you never come back?"

Her mother sighed heavily again. "I could not do as I wished to. That is all. I had nothing. I only had . . . " She hesitated. "Georgiana, I remarried. My husband would not have you, but he would pay for the school. I had no choice."

"But you wrote and said you could no longer pay."

"Mr. Gamble died, and there was not enough money

left. It broke my heart, dear; truly it did; but what I did was best for you. I had to find a way to support myself, and I knew you would do much better if you stayed at the school . . . and away from me."

Georgiana breathed in deeply, taking in her mother's familiar scent. "I do not think I am better off, Mother."

"Nonsense. Just look at how you are dressed! I could never have done that for you. I should have made it impossible for you to hold your head up."

"It is not what you think. I am still plain Miss Marland. I am still ineligible."

"And who has told you that?"

"I know it is true." She paused and then looked up into her mother's face. "Lady Estcott has taken me in."

"Lady Estcott?"

"Yes. Her great-nephew, Lord Ryburn, told me that she once refused to help you. And now you are here, and I am with Lady Estcott, and I still cannot marry the man I love."

Her mother stared into her eyes, then straightened and returned to her dressing table chair. But now, she did not touch the powder, but continued to regard her daughter.

"You do not realize how hard my life has been. It is not a life you would have liked to lead. I could not have allowed it if there was any way to prevent it, and there was a way." She hesitated. "It gives me great joy to know that your fate is better than mine. It may not be perfect, but no life is. I want that better life for you, Georgiana. And I want it for your father's daughter."

Georgiana sat there silently and digested her mother's words . . . and she remembered someone else's. *Why would she not be in touch with you? She may wish to protect you. She may not want you to know what her circumstances are.*

The words were Lord Ryburn's.

"So . . . tell me who this young man is whom you wish to marry and cannot."

Georgiana blinked and met her mother's gaze.

"It does not matter at all, Mother, for he is Lady Estcott's great-nephew. He is a viscount now, and will inherit an earldom someday. I have not a hope."

Her mother's eyes widened. "Lord Ryburn."

"Yes."

A knock sounded on her door. "My lady, may I enter the castle?" came a jovial voice.

"Oh, not now," muttered her mother. "Georgiana—quickly. Into the wardrobe—hurry!"

Her mother flung open the doors of her wardrobe, stuffed to overflowing with dresses on hooks. She madly grabbed an armload of gowns, flung them over the back of a chair, and grabbed Georgiana's arm. "Get in—quickly!"

Georgiana stepped in; her mother gave her a not-so-gentle push and slammed the doors shut behind her.

"Mrs. Gaaar-son . . ."

"One moment!"

Georgiana heard the door open.

"I thought I was being excluded, my dear."

"You should not be here, and the answer is no."

"What? Have I done anything to deserve such treatment?"

"No, but you are about to!"

"You have another friend?"

"Do not be so foolish. Here, come in; but you cannot stay long."

Georgiana heard a man's heavy step, and struggled with the familiarity of his voice. She pressed her eye to a crack in the door. Unfortunately, she could see nothing at the moment but her mother's back where she had reseated herself at the dressing table.

"You have him hiding in here, perhaps?" His voice still had a tone of playfulness in it.

"Dear sir, if I looked until I was old and gray and fit for no one, I should not find another gentleman as worthy as you. That is not it at all. This is simply not a good time."

"Perhaps if you tell me why?"

"Thank you for the flowers," she said dismissively.

"I should love to do more, but you will not allow me to. I have never met another woman such as you, Gloriane."

"Of course I do not believe that."

"But it is true. You take nothing. I am at my wit's end."

"And if I took something, what then? You would expect something in return, and you would be very distressed with me when I did not give it to you."

"You wrong me deeply."

He moved again, stepping forward several paces, and Georgiana glimpsed his face at last.

It was Lord Wyndgrave.

Georgiana felt her throat tighten. *Mother and Lord Wyndgrave. And here she was trapped in the wardrobe!*

Lord Wyndgrave bent down and pressed a kiss on top of her mother's head. "You will accept another drive, will you not?"

"Yes, as long as it is in an open carriage."

"As you wish. You so enjoyed our last foray into the country. . . . I never saw you look so lovely."

"You really must go now."

Another knock sounded on the door.

"There! I have competition!" Lord Wyndgrave said. "Who is it?"

For an answer, the door simply opened. A pause . . . and then she heard, "Mrs. Garson . . . Father."

Hugh closed the door, and Georgiana heard him sigh. "Mrs. Garson . . . I am in search of Miss Marland. I thought that perhaps she had come your way."

"Miss Marland?" asked Lord Wyndgrave.

"Yes. She is attending tonight with Aunt Estcott, Lord Felstone, and me, and she has vanished."

"I have not seen her, Hugh," said Lord Wyndgrave.

"Have you seen her, Miss Garson?" He paused. *"Mrs. Marland?"*

"What?" said Lord Wyndgrave.

Georgiana heard her mother sigh heavily. "Does anyone else know who I am, Lord Ryburn?"

"Not to my knowledge."

Her mother rose, came forward, and flung the wardrobe open. "Come out, dear. As you know, we have company."

Georgiana brushed aside a plume of ostrich feathers that was dangling down and gave an explosive sneeze.

Chapter Twelve

"*M*iss Marland!" exclaimed both gentlemen at once.

Georgiana stepped out of the wardrobe and stood in her mother's tiny dressing room, necessarily in close proximity to her mother, Lord Wyndgrave, and Lord Ryburn.

"I can explain," she said weakly.

"Lord Wyndgrave, I now have something to ask of you," said Georgiana's mother. "Miss Marland . . . is my daughter. I beg of you, do not reveal this to anybody."

He was silent for a long moment, gazing at the former Mrs. Marland, then at Georgiana, and then at Mrs. Marland once more with an uncharacteristically somber look. Then he said, "Did you believe that I did not know? From the first time I took you driving in the country, I have seen you without your costume and paint and wig. I only had to meet Miss Marland to know she is your daughter."

"Father, is that true?"

Lord Wyndgrave turned to his son. "It is. I saw no reason to mention it. Clearly Miss Marland grew up in the young ladies' academy, and one could assume her mother did not have much in the way of means, particularly as she chose to disappear. I felt that the fewer persons who knew the details of Miss Garson's past, the better for the both of them."

Lord Ryburn sighed. "Father, matters are more complicated than you understand."

"And how is that?"

"They are more complicated than *you* understand, Lord Ryburn," said Georgiana's mother. Then she looked at Lord Wyndgrave. "Does the possibility not exist that your son and my daughter may . . . have an attachment?"

Lord Wyndgrave looked astonished. Then, he laughed. "Upon my soul! Hugh, is this the case?"

Lord Ryburn was frowning. "Nothing so humorous as that, Father." He then turned his frown on Georgiana.

"Coming here was most unwise. Your absence has now been remarked, and who knows who may have seen you come this way. We must leave as soon as possible—and as quietly and circumspectly as possible."

Georgiana gazed at him, her hurt overflowing. "Do

not worry, I am leaving immediately." She stepped forward and attempted to pass the two men, but Lord Ryburn stopped her.

"Do not be foolish."

"It is you who are being foolish. Take your hand from me and let me pass." She glared at him. He stared back, and suddenly he released her. She quickly opened the door, scanned the hall, and stepped out.

Georgiana's vision blurred from the tears in her eyes, but she took care to be as cautious as she could, at last making her way to the powder room where she could repair the damage from her adventure. She wondered how she was to return to the box when Lady Estcott and Lord Felstone must be fretting with worry for her, but there was no help for it. She only hoped her absence had not been noted by anyone else.

She stepped from the powder room only to encounter Lord Ryburn's furious face. He immediately caught her arm. "Let us walk as though nothing were wrong," he said tightly.

And so they did, all the way back to the box, and it seemed the ploy was successful. Georgiana never knew that a pair of sharp eyes had noted much more than she realized.

The first rumor reached Hugh on the following day. He went to White's for dinner, which was often his custom when not otherwise engaged, and immediately noted a quickly stilled conversation when he walked up to the table where his friend, Lord Winston, was seated. Hugh also recognized the quietly guarded look in Winny's eyes.

"Sit down, Ryburn," Winny said cheerfully. "Weston and Banover have just been discussing a rather interesting bit of gossip."

Lord Banover grunted. "I only heard it. I did not say it was interesting." He glanced uncomfortably at his pocket watch. "Must be going. Sorry to have to dash. Good night, gentlemen."

"I must as well," said Weston.

"What?" said Winny. "The matter might be settled here and now, and instead you are all leaving."

"My apologies," said Weston. He stood and walked away.

Hugh pulled out a chair and sat down. "Very well. Tell me about it."

Winny gave him a wry look. "Sorry, old fellow, but the fox is among the hens now. Someone is saying that Gloriane Garson is Miss Marland's mother."

Hugh closed his eyes briefly and sighed.

"I of course will repeat nothing, and I certainly will do my best to help, if there is any way I can."

"Find out who is saying this. The source of the rumor."

"I can try." He paused, then said quietly, "It is not true, is it?"

Hugh looked at his friend. "Imagine, if you will, that it were true. Now consider what I would say."

"Absolutely nothing."

"And if it were not?"

"I imagine you would deny it straight out."

"Then you have your answer. Pray do not repeat it."

"It is rather hard to repeat nothing, old fellow."

"Precisely."

Winny took a sip of his wine, then rested the glass on the table and studied it, turning the goblet around and around by the stem. "Odd. They don't look much like mother and daughter."

"No."

"That certainly seems to belie the rumor."

"It is not enough."

Winny continued to study his glass; then he said, "I suppose another woman could not come forward and claim to be Mrs. Marland."

"An entertaining idea, but completely absurd. Still, thank you for trying."

Hugh left White's with no further useful information, and with no better ideas on how to squelch the rumor. He turned his rig toward Park Lane, not wishing for the unpleasantness that was about to rain down upon him, but not wishing to postpone it.

Upon his arrival, he learned that Lady Estcott had a visitor. Lord Felstone was sitting in the drawing room with Hugh's aunt and Miss Marland, all of them enjoying a cup of tea after dinner.

"How pleasant to see you, Hugh," said his aunt. "You have missed Miss Frey—she retired to her room already. It is somewhat late to call."

Hugh made his usual greeting and sat between Lady Estcott and Miss Marland.

"I am afraid I have something rather private to convey," he said. "It concerns Miss Marland."

Everyone stared at him. His aunt Estcott spoke first.

"Then speak. You need not be concerned about Lord Felstone. He is the soul of discretion."

"Miss Marland should perhaps be the one to decide," said Hugh.

"I am about to leave anyway. We have had a wonderful dinner, and I am just finishing my tea."

"No, do not go, Lord Felstone." Georgiana looked at Hugh. "Lord Felstone may stay. He is a friend."

"Do not keep us waiting, Hugh." Aunt Estcott eyed him steadily, waiting.

"A rumor is about that Gloriane Garson is Miss Marland's mother."

Aunt Estcott and Lord Felstone looked astonished. Georgiana's face paled, and she looked down at her teacup.

"What rubbish!" cried Lady Estcott.

"Shocking," said Lord Felstone.

"As yet I do not know how it started," Hugh said. "But I shall learn."

Lady Estcott sniffed regally, her eyes blazing. "Well, *I* know who is responsible. Look no farther than Lady Etherington. She wished to cause me trouble, and now she has."

"I do not think a mutual dislike is reason enough," Hugh said.

"I am afraid it may well be true," said Lord Felstone. "She told me directly that she planned to see what she could learn about Miss Marland. She hinted that she believed there was something undesirable to learn about her mother."

"I knew it!" sputtered Lady Estcott. "I knew she would cause trouble! As soon as you told me, Lord Felstone, I knew I must be on my guard!"

"Abominable, that is what it is," said Felstone.

"Attacking an innocent girl out of spite!" replied Aunt Estcott. "Well, what is to be done about it? I hope you have put it about that it is not true?"

Hugh looked at Miss Marland. She was sitting very still, yet staring at her cup. She seemed to sense his gaze, though, and looked up to meet it. Her blue eyes were full of sorrow. Then she turned to his aunt.

"He cannot say that it is not true," she said quietly, "because it is."

Aunt Estcott stared at her in shocked bewilderment. "What do you mean? Are you saying that Gloriane Garson is your *mother*?"

"Yes, I am."

Lady Estcott hesitated. "And you did not tell *me*?"

"No. But I only learned myself on the night of the ball."

Miss Marland thought she could die a thousand times beneath Lady Estcott's glare, but she held her chin up. Georgiana owed her the truth, such as it was.

Lady Estcott turned her gaze back upon her nephew. "And *you* knew, as well?"

"I learned the night of the ball, as did Miss Marland." He appeared uncomfortable, regretful, and tired. Between the last look he had given her, asking her what he should say, and her decision to tell the truth, he had not looked at her again.

"Did *everyone* but *I* learn the night of the ball?"

"No, only Miss Marland and I."

"I think not. Someone else knows about it now, that is clear!"

Lord Felstone cleared his throat. "Lady Etherington was at the ball, as well as at the theater last night."

At that, Lady Estcott gazed at her old friend, and her shoulders sagged. "I am undone," she said.

"Never, my dear," said Lord Felstone. "We shall come about."

Georgiana swallowed. "I am sorry, Lady Estcott."

The lady looked at her with eyes that were sharp and hurt. "Do not speak!" she snapped. "I had rather you said nothing at all!"

Georgiana sat still but for a moment, then rose and left the room.

Hugh rode to his father's home the next morning, determined to have a serious discussion. He fully expected to find him in his morning undress with his dog, but found him in the garden with a pistol instead, taking practice shots at a paper target.

"Father, I must speak to you."

"Good morning, son. One moment."

Hugh wisely waited until his father squeezed off the next shot before he spoke again.

His father turned, noticed his son's face, and excused his servant.

"Tell me what it is," he said, in that patient tone usually reserved for a recalcitrant child.

They walked toward the terrace together while Hugh explained the matter of Miss Marland and her mother.

"Those gossips. They must always be picking for some way to make trouble for another."

They sat on the terrace, and Lord Wyndgrave sent for a pot of tea. Then he sat back and gazed at Hugh.

"Son, some things have no easy solution. Society will do as it wills. That is why it is wise not to consider it so very important. I ceased to do so long ago. Your great-aunt, unfortunately, values it highly, and it is of some importance to your Miss Marland."

"*My* Miss Marland? That is not worthy of you."

He shrugged. "It is important to her, in any case, because Aunt Estcott has made it so. Now, it is different for Gloriane. The gossip may even help her popularity, but it will break her heart to injure her daughter."

"And what if it is revealed that Gloriane Garson is having an affair with you?"

His father's eyes shuttered, but his lips smiled. "That is the odd thing. We are not having an affair. I have courted her with an eye toward one, but she would have none of it. Says she must be married, and in the same breath tells me she would love to go driving with me. Yet, I am sure she would abandon me in an instant for her principles."

"No one would believe your relationship is chaste."

"Exactly! Not with *my* reputation! I wonder at it, myself."

"The news would hurt Aunt Estcott and Miss Marland even more."

His father frowned. "Are you suggesting that I should no longer see Gloriane? For if you are, I am not prepared to go as far as *that*. I am deuced fond of the woman—more so than I have been of any female in a devil of a long time."

"Perhaps she will feel differently about seeing you once she knows that her daughter's welfare is at stake."

His father swore. "Son, I do not pry into your private life. I shall tell you this but once: Do not interfere with mine!"

"I will not. I do not have to utter a word for Miss Marland's mother to learn the gossip. I am only suggesting how it will be."

His father, frowning, sat back in his chair. At last he said, "You might consider taking some action yourself. Marry the girl."

Hugh stared. "You mean Miss Marland?"

"Well, I certainly do not mean her mother! Hell's bells, Son, wake up! Your life is wasting away! You have been ready to lay your fate into the hands of that Miss—Miss—whatever her name is, Hartley—and you cannot even consider the woman who makes your blood flow through your veins!"

Hugh lifted his tea and took a long sip, then rested his cup. "I never thought of it. She is ineligible. Aunt Estcott never hinted of the possibility, for all that she was trying to make Miss Marland pass in society."

"She got the girl into Almack's. I am beginning to think that you both are nicked in the bob."

"She will not be in Almack's after today, I fear."

"It doesn't matter. What matters is that she is a decent girl, and presuming you love her—whether she has money or not, is loved by society or not—what does all that matter to you? You do not need either."

Hugh frowned. "Women are fleeting. You have taught me that yourself. Love invites loss. I intend never to fall in love and then spend half my life grieving over it." He then rose from the table, hoping he had given his father a great deal to think about.

Chapter Thirteen

"**D**on't just stand there and stare at me, Hugh! She has gone off, and I have no idea where it is she has gone. She left me the note and nearly all her clothes—and that is all I know!"

Hugh sat with his distraught Aunt Estcott in the small drawing room. She had arisen from her bed, where she had stayed for the past several days, to meet with him. With them were Lord Felstone and Miss Frey, who looked as though she had been crying.

"Did she say anything to indicate why she might leave?"

"She felt she had caused us all trouble," said Miss Frey.

"Which she did," exclaimed Aunt Estcott, "but I did not want her to leave!"

"Perhaps she did not realize that, Aunt Estcott."

"Do not chastise me, Hugh! I simply want her found." Aunt Estcott drew a handkerchief from her pocket and wiped her nose. Lord Felstone patted her knee.

"She is not at the young ladies' academy," said Lord Felstone. "I sent a man over there to check."

"Let me think," said Hugh. For a moment there was silence, but it did not serve to help him at all.

Miss Marland knew that there was no position waiting for her at Miss Silby's Academy. He was not aware of any other friends or acquaintances she might have made who could be of help to her, save those in this room. She was upset, it was certain, but she was not foolish. She would not leave with nowhere to go.

There was a slim chance she might go to his father, he thought suddenly. Yes, that was a distinct possibility.

"Send a note to my father, to see if she might have gone there."

"An excellent idea," Felstone said.

"I shall write immediately," said Lady Estcott.

"Perhaps *I* should," said Hugh. "No—I do not know. If she is there, my father might think he is protecting her from one of us."

"Ridiculous," said his aunt. "It is a family matter, and we all share in her welfare." She rang her bell, and quickly dispatched the servant to bring her writing box.

"I hope she is safe," murmured Miss Frey. "Poor child, losing both parents and growing up alone."

Hugh felt worse and worse, and the guilt began to throb inside him like a wound. He might have taken care of her; he might have asked her to marry him. But it had been ingrained in him to make a business out of marriage and never to depend upon love.

The fact was that it was too late. He had spent the last three days thinking about his father's advice, and had realized that he was in love with Miss Marland. He just did not know if she could ever love him. Could he live with her as his wife, if he knew she did not return his affection? The thought had stopped him cold . . . and now, Miss Marland was gone.

The servant returned with the writing box, and Lady Estcott began to hastily scratch out a note. "Fetch a footman," she commanded the servant. "I need this delivered to Lord Wyndgrave immediately!"

The letter was folded, sealed, and dispatched, and the four were left to look at each other again.

"What will you do now, Hugh," asked his aunt, "other than sit there looking like a stepped-upon pup?"

"I am trying to decide, Aunt."

"I am as well," said Felstone.

More silence. Hugh found himself staring at the

empty pianoforte, with a faint echo of a Haydn sonata playing in his head.

There was a sudden sound at the drawing room door and it opened. Through the doorway stepped Miss Marland.

Hugh leapt to his feet. "Miss Marland!"

"Where have you been?" cried Aunt Estcott. "We have been beside ourselves!"

Miss Marland came forward, then stopped, looking from Hugh to Aunt Estcott and back to Hugh. "I am sorry," she said breathlessly. "I am sorry, but . . . my mother is missing!"

"Your mother?" asked Lord Ryburn.

Miss Marland gazed at him, all the while aware of how she looked in her old day gown and bonnet. She wished that she was somehow more presentable, but there was nothing for it. She could only worry now for her mother, and her deepest fear was that she could not convince Lady Estcott—or Lord Ryburn—to help her.

"Yes. I—I went to the Theatre Royal, you see, for I . . . well, I thought that was the best possible place for me to start over. I thought my mother could help me, and I do have my music."

She nearly winced at the horrified expression on Lady Estcott's face.

"And then what happened?" asked Lord Ryburn.

He, surprisingly enough, did not look shocked or angry. He simply stared at her, as if he was afraid she would vanish from sight.

"I was told that Gloriane Garson had gone. That she had packed her bags and left after her performance last night."

Hugh closed his eyes briefly and then opened them again. She wondered what he was thinking. He felt compassion for her, she knew, but he might possibly be thinking of his father, as well.

"Did she leave any information behind?"

"No. That is why I—I wish for help. The note said she would not return, and that was all."

"I will see what I can discover," Lord Ryburn said.

"Please," said Lady Estcott, "go change out of that dreadful gown and put on one of your new frocks. And never give me a scare like this again!"

Georgiana looked at the circle of concerned faces and felt the tears start to her eyes.

"I shall, Lady Estcott. Thank you. Thank you all very much."

She returned to her room, her heart a curious mix of happiness and sadness. In spite of it all, she was home, surrounded by people who cared about her.

Her relief lasted until dinnertime, when she came downstairs to learn that a note that Lady Estcott had sent to Lord Wyndgrave had been brought back without a reply.

*   *   *

Lord Ryburn called the next day, and he asked to see Georgiana.

Georgiana met him in the library and was surprised to see him draw the door closed behind them.

"Have you found my mother?" The serious expression on his face terrified her so much that her hands were trembling.

"Sit down, Miss Marland."

"No! Not until you tell me—"

"Please. Sit down. This is not about your mother."

She sat slowly, her eyes never leaving his face. "What is it?"

He drew a breath. "Miss Marland, I have thought of a fair solution to our difficulties. You shall be secure, matters will improve for my aunt, and your mother will no longer need to worry about you." He paused.

Georgiana wondered if he was really going to say what she was thinking, but that seemed wholly impossible. "Go on."

"As you know, I have no need of money. My aunt's money makes no difference to me. I also live quite happily not worrying overly much about society." He hesitated a long moment, gazing at her face. Then he said, "Miss Marland, would you consent to be my wife?"

Georgiana stared. Then she realized her mouth was open, which he had very kindly not mentioned.

"Lord Ryburn—I—I could not possibly! You are all but engaged to Miss Hartley, and I will bring you disgrace. I could not sacrifice you for my own comfort. And Lady Estcott! She could not possibly approve. You are kind, indeed, you are excessively kind—but I could not. . . ."

She could not read the emotion that flickered over his face. "Miss Marland, you are not responsible for my decisions."

"And you, Lord Ryburn, are not responsible for mine."

He continued to stare at her for a long moment. At last he said, "Do not refuse me out of hand. If I did not want to marry you, I should not have asked. Say no more now—but please consider my proposal."

With that he made a little bow and left her in the library.

Georgiana took a few minutes to compose herself, then rose and walked out into the entrance hall. The butler, Dawes, on his way to the stairs with a silver salver in his hand, saw her and changed his direction.

"Miss Marland, a letter for you."

Georgiana took the letter, and immediately recognized her mother's hand on the address. Hurriedly she tore it open.

My Dearest Daughter,
I am writing to tell you that I have gone away to

get married. Do not fret. It is the very best solution, and I am very happy. I shall allow my husband to announce the news when we return, but I did not want you to worry.

I also want you to know that Gloriane Garson will cease to be, and you shall be free to pursue your own happiness.

All my love,
Mother

Georgiana let out a little cry, and then she thought of the one other person who needed to hear this news.

"Lord Ryburn!" She hurried up the hallway. "Dawes! Has Lord Ryburn left?"

"I do not believe he has. I believe he has gone to the small drawing room to see her ladyship."

Georgiana darted up the stairs and, arriving breathless at the top, continued her rush to the drawing room and flung open the door. "Lord Ryburn, are you here?"

Lady Estcott, Lord Felstone, Miss Frey, and Lord Ryburn all looked up in surprise.

"Oh—I am sorry to have rushed in so, but—" She held the note in the air. "From my mother. Lord Ryburn, I think you should see what you can make of it."

He rose and came up to her, took the note from her hand, and read it. He frowned and read it again.

"What is it?" said Lady Estcott. "I wish to know,

too! I do have an interest in things other than my pending ruin at the hands of gossips."

"Dear, you shall not be ruined," murmured Felstone.

"I know that. I am only disgusted over the matter. Hugh has yet to be married, and there is poor Miss Marland with no prospects. It is all too aggravating."

Hugh stood with his back to the group, so only Georgiana could see his face. He lifted his eyes to hers. "My father has married her," he said quietly.

"I was afraid of that," Georgiana said sadly. "Can you ever forgive my mother and me for what we have done?"

He folded the note and handed it back to her. "You have done nothing, save live, and my father is very capable of making choices for himself. I think your mother may suit him admirably."

"You cannot mean that."

"Why can I not?" His golden eyes spoke volumes.

"What is it?" called Lady Estcott again.

Lord Ryburn answered her without taking his eyes from Georgiana's face. "It seems that Gloriane Garson has married. We shall find out to whom she is married in a day or two."

The gossip mill was busy with the disappearance of Gloriane Garson. A number of speculations were passed about, a couple of them quite outrageous, but all agreed that she had gone off with a lover.

As for Georgiana's reputation, she had attended no events since the ball and the party at Lord Wyndgrave's, and invitations had vanished. Lady Estcott suffered with snubs, as well, although she did not speak of them; but Lord Felstone was now a daily visitor, and his steady presence seemed to be slowly and surely filling the void in Lady Estcott's life.

Georgiana waited every day for news of her mother. She also waited every day in hopes of a visit from Lord Ryburn. It had been four days now since his proposal and the letter from her mother, and he had returned twice for news. She dearly hoped that today would be one of the days he would come.

An arrival was announced just as they were about to go down for the evening meal. Lady Estcott, who normally would express decided annoyance at such an imposition, instead impatiently demanded that Dawes read her the visiting card.

"It says 'Lord and Lady Wyndgrave,' your ladyship."

"Lord and Lady . . . ? Dawes, bring me the card!"

"Shall I bring them up, madam?" Dawes walked across the drawing room to her and held out the salver. Lady Estcott snatched the card and looked at it, and Georgiana stood up to view it over her shoulder. It was indeed Lord Wyndgrave's card, but the two words "and Lady" had been added to it in a flourishing hand.

"Yes, bring them up."

Georgiana returned to her chair and waited with a hammering heart. The door opened at last, and in stepped Lord Wyndgrave and a slender, dark haired lady in a pretty yellow muslin gown and a deep green pelisse, fresh faced and smiling, without a trace of powder or rouge.

Georgiana stared; then she jumped up with a cry and ran to her.

"Mother!" She hugged the pretty, slender woman she remembered, and Lady Wyndgrave hugged her back.

"I thought you would not know me," she joked.

"Mother, if I know you padded and painted in a blond wig, I certainly know you now!"

Lady Estcott herself rose to her feet. "You are Miss Marland's mother?"

"Why, yes I am. I have been Mrs. Gamble until four days ago, when your nephew and I were married."

Lady Estcott continued to stare at Lady Wyndgrave in confusion, and Lord Wyndgrave stood beside his wife, grinning in amusement.

"Your daughter looks very much like you," said Lady Estcott at last. Then she added, "But I thought Georgiana's mother was Gloriane Garson."

Both Lord Wyndgrave and his wife laughed then, and, observing the others, Georgiana saw Miss Frey's mouth form an O of surprise, which she delicately covered with one hand.

Lord Felstone was next to understand, and Lady Estcott was the very last.

Lady Wyndgrave walked up to Lady Estcott and stopped before her. "I do beg your pardon, Lady Estcott. I did not want to tease, but your nephew was quite set upon it. You see, I *was* Gloriane Garson, but it was only a stage name, and I always took care to wear an elaborate costume. I had a daughter to protect, and I did not want her mother to be recognized on stage."

"My heavens." Lady Estcott began to sink back into her chair. "Marigold, bring me my vinaigrette."

Miss Frey was at her side in a trice, holding the vial under her ladyship's nose.

"Are you quite all right, Lady Estcott?" asked Lady Wyndgrave. "Oh, I am so sorry. Lord Wyndgrave, see how we have shocked your aunt!"

Georgiana's heart was full. She already knew how it was to be. Gloriane Garson was gone, and no one would see her again; now there was her mother, looking years younger and as happy as a girl.

"You will not sing again?" asked Lady Estcott.

"No, I shall not. Oh, perhaps for my closest family I shall, but from this day forward Gloriane Garson is no more, and Miss Marland's real mother has returned."

"I expect Gloriane Garson has gone to sing on the Continent," said Lord Wyndgrave jokingly.

"No one will know you as Gloriane Garson," said

Lady Estcott. "I can hardly believe it. The rumors will stop; there will be no scandal. . . ."

Georgiana heard the sound of the door behind her, and she turned toward it. In walked Lord Ryburn, his face alive with curiosity.

"Lord Ryburn," Georgiana said, "please do come and meet my mother, Lady Wyndgrave."

She could see that he was every bit as impressed with Gloriane Garson's transformation to Lady Wyndgrave, the former Mrs. Gamble, as she was.

"So you see, there will be no more scandal," she said to him, "and you need have no worry for me."

His gaze returned to her face, and she almost thought he looked sad. But then, her eyes were misting, and she could not trust that she was seeing him so very clearly.

Chapter Fourteen

*H*er world had changed yet again.

She was still Lady Estcott's ward, but the invitations started to come again, more numerous than before. The odd story of Gloriane Garson was talked about everywhere. Occasionally someone still wondered why she had been thought to be Miss Marland's mother—and the occasional person stubbornly held on to the belief that she was—but for the most part the scandal died like the wind after a passing storm, and it was no more than an entertaining story.

But the greatest change of all was that she had her mother again after three lonely years—even longer if she counted all the years she had been at Miss Silby's when she saw her mother infrequently and only for brief encounters. She had all this now, and for the first time since she had come to Lady Estcott's, her fears were gone.

There was only one shadow in her life. . . . Every day, she wondered if she would hear of the engagement of Lord Ryburn and Miss Hartley.

She had scarcely seen Lord Ryburn since her mother's marriage to his father. It was much more likely now that she saw Lord Wyndgrave than him; and although Lord Wyndgrave was cheerful and gallant and made her mother happy, every time he looked at her mother, Georgiana remembered that special warmth she had seen in Lord Ryburn's eyes.

A month had passed, then two, and the season was growing old. There were several young men who called on her, but as to whom she might choose, Lady Estcott offered no suggestion. She was oddly as casual now about the matter as she had once been passionate; her only comment was that Georgiana must not be in too much of a hurry, for a good husband was worth waiting for.

On this late June morning Georgiana sat in the drawing room with Lady Estcott and Miss Frey, embroidering lace handkerchiefs with her mother's new initials, when she heard the sound of a new arrival in the hall. The door opened, and she heard a familiar voice, one she no longer expected to hear.

"Good morning, Aunt Estcott. Miss Frey. Miss Marland."

She made every effort not to seem overly eager, but when his eyes met hers, she melted inside.

"Lord Ryburn. I had thought you had forgotten all about us."

"No. I have only been busy. I understand things are going well for you."

She knew that he meant with the social whirl and the beaux who called upon her. She wished he knew that those things were not important to her, and that the prospect of choosing a husband had lost its charm for her.

As she did not answer him immediately, Lady Estcott answered for her. "It has been going very well. She has turned down two proposals in the last month."

"I thought that perhaps you might like to take a drive, Miss Marland," he said.

It was remarkable how her heart lifted at those words, how her entire being suddenly felt light and happy. *Perhaps he means to tell me about Miss Hartley*, she thought, then chastised herself for thinking it. "I should love to go!"

Georgiana changed as quickly as possible for the ride with the help of Susan, who was now quite the competent abigail. Susan made sure her bonnet was tied just so and that she carried a warmer shawl in case the weather turned. Soon Lord Ryburn was handing her into his phaeton.

"I thought we might go walking in Green Park. I remember you have a preference for it."

As they traveled along Park Lane toward Green Park, Georgiana remembered the sadness of another occasion when she had been driving with Lord Ryburn, and how she had wished she could feel simple pleasure like the fashionable persons she saw walking, instead of worrying. She realized she was closer to feeling that way now than she had ever thought possible. Perhaps, she thought, she would never be completely happy, but she would be ungrateful indeed to complain of her circumstances now.

They drove into Green Park, and Lord Ryburn assisted her out of the carriage and turned the reins over to his tiger. He then took a flat rectangular parcel from the phaeton and turned to her, offering his arm.

"Believe it or not, I have missed our dancing lessons," he said. His topaz eyes twinkled in the sunlight, and she smiled back at him.

"I know very well that you did not enjoy them but thank you all the same."

"I did not realize how much I would miss seeing you," he said. His expression had sobered, and she heard wistfulness in his voice.

"You said you have been busy," she said, hoping he did not notice her sudden nervousness.

"I have been, and I have brought the fruit of my labors to show you."

"Really?" She looked at the paper-wrapped parcel under his arm.

"Yes. Let us go sit on the bench under that tree."

He placed the parcel in her arms once they had seated themselves. "Open it."

She tore at the paper eagerly, and the parcel soon revealed a wooden frame. The rest of the paper came away, and she gazed down at what he had brought.

It was a perfectly rendered drawing, in delicate and sensitive detail, of her own face.

She gazed at it, and her eyes misted.

"Do you like it?"

She sniffed quietly. "Very much."

"What is wrong?"

"Nothing at all."

"There is something. Please tell me."

She looked at the face of the man she loved, and saw that his eyes were questioning and concerned.

"You drew my portrait . . . so you can always have me, even after I am gone."

He still seemed puzzled. "Why does it make you sad?"

She looked at the portrait again. "You already think of me as gone away, like your mother. And I remember you told me that a likeness is the only thing you can truly keep."

He cleared his throat. "I think I did say that. But I do not think that was what I meant. The portrait contains a memory, but the subject is more precious.

It is just that subjects, unlike portraits, tend to go away."

"And so you have been afraid to trust your heart, for fear of breaking it."

"Is that what it means?"

"I do not know. Only you know the answer." She looked back at him, gazing deeply into his golden eyes, wanting to remember them the way they looked today. "I do know that you are courting Miss Hartley, and I do not think you are in love with her. I know that you asked me to marry you, and said not one word of love—only of keeping me safe."

For a moment he did not respond, and then he sighed. "Perhaps you have found me out. I have not loved a woman before, not since I lost my mother. I simply did not think about why."

"Then you love someone now?"

His eyelids lowered slightly. "Miss Marland, I have spent weeks drawing your portrait and have come all this way to give it to you. And I am giving it to you because I do not want the portrait. I want the woman I drew. I am in love with you, Miss Marland."

"You are?"

"Yes. I cannot be satisfied with your likeness. I should a thousand times rather have you no matter how much I may fear losing you, for it is too late. I am deeply and irrevocably in love with you."

"Oh—oh, Lord Ryburn."

"Will you marry me?"

She sighed, "Yes. Oh, yes!"

He smiled then, and it was as if the sun had driven the last of the clouds away. "You may now call me 'Hugh,' " he said.

"Yes, Lord Ryburn."

"Yes, Hugh," he said. And then he leaned very close and kissed her on the lips.

A moment later, the portrait slipped from Georgiana's lap onto the grass, but both teacher and student were so engaged that neither of them noticed it.

Epilogue

*F*ew were surprised when Miss Hartley's engagement to Lord Strathmore was announced. Lady Hartley told her friends that her daughter had tired of Lord Ryburn not paying her proper attention. It did cause some speculation, however, when Miss Marland's engagement to the supposedly inattentive Lord Ryburn soon followed.

Some concluded that Miss Marland was less particular, given her status. Some considered it a match of convenience, as Miss Marland was somehow a distant relative of the family and the ward of Lord Ryburn's great-aunt. But those who were close to the couple knew it was a love match and were very glad of it.

The season of surprises was not over, however, for the biggest surprise of all came last. Lady Estcott married Lord Felstone on a warm day in autumn, and it was the talk of the town for weeks to come.

"A delightful new writer!"
—Edith Layton

DECEIVING
MISS DEARBORN
by
Laurie Bishop

When Miss Annabelle Dearborn opens
her doors to boarders, she meets a
handsome stranger—a man with no
memory, but one with the markings of
nobility. As they begin to fall for one
another, this man of mystery prays
he's worthy of her love—once he
learns who he really is.

0-451-21014-X

**Available wherever books are
sold or at penguin.com**

Now available from
REGENCY ROMANCE

Marry in Haste and Francesca's Rake
by Lynn Kerstan
Together for the first time, two Regency classics star
heroines gambling on love, not knowing if they will
lose their hearts—or win true love.
0-451-21717-9

Miss Clarkson's Classmate
by Sharon Sobel
Emily Clarkson arrives at her new teaching position
expecting her employer to be a gentleman, and she's
shocked to find a brute. He's expecting a somber old
maid. And neither is expecting the passion that soon
overtakes them both.
0-451-21718-7

Lady Emma's Dilemma
by Rhonda Woodward
Once lovers, Lady Emmaline and Baron Devreux have
different points of view concerning their long-ago
tryst. But in an unexpected encounter, the two simply
have too many questions and the answers only come
by moonlight—and with a little mischief.
0-451-21701-2